❁ ❁

Joe and Mr. Penny had worked hard and created a beautiful garden at the back of the junkyard. It meant everything
to them—a refuge from the dirty streets and dilapidated
buildings around them in London, a home for their animals,
and a place of peace and friendship.

Then, suddenly, their private world was threatened by
what Mr. Penny called "progress." It seemed that everyone
wanted to bulldoze the entire area in order to redevelop.
The most insistent offer came from Mr. Massiter, who just
couldn't see that the beautiful garden was worth preserving.

Joe just had to do something. So he took his pet weasel
and went to see Mr. Massiter and that was the beginning . . .

A Small Piece of Paradise is a very special story about
values and understanding and growing up. In a world
oriented toward change, it points out again that people are
more important than material things and that their hopes
and dreams make the world a better place.

A Small Piece of Paradise

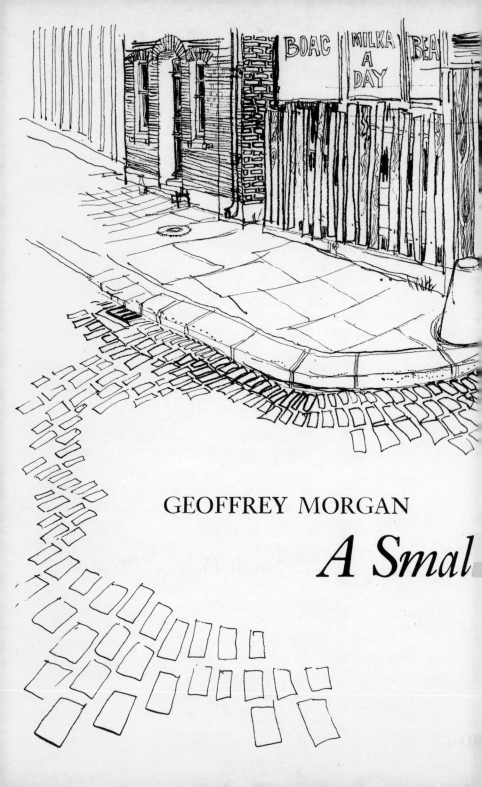

GEOFFREY MORGAN

A Smal

J.J. PENNY & SON
Second-hand dealer

Piece of Paradise

Illustrated by DAVID KNIGHT

ALFRED A. KNOPF · NEW YORK

SEA-TITLE II

for Gladys and Reg

A Small Piece of Paradise

· Chapter One ·

Joe would never forget the day it all started. Liz was having measles and Aunt Ethel was having a baby, and outside Mr. Penny's front door stood a shiny Rolls-Royce. It was long and black, with a dark-suited driver, like you see at funerals, only the man who came out of Mr. Penny's house didn't have a top hat.

Joe stood, shuffling his feet on the uneven flagstones as the stranger entered the car and it glided away down Sparrow Street. He watched it disappear behind the blank wall of the old trolley depot, then he turned toward the double gates in the creosote fence below the line of billboards.

The billboards were the one splash of color visible in Sparrow Street. They drew your attention because the pictures were nicer to look at than the empty toy factory on the opposite side of the road. Above the gates there was already a drawing of a pretty girl with not much on. She advertised the coming attraction at the Hippodrome. Every week the bill-sticker came and pasted a label across her legs announcing the current feature. Next to her was the huge face of a boy brushing his teeth with Maclean's, and the next told what was showing at the Roxy. The one right at the end showed a man with a house over his head in the shape of an umbrella. It had something to do with insurance. But Joe never could get the message.

Still, the pictures weren't bad really, and they always put clean ones up when the old ones got dirty or passers-by disfigured them with penciled remarks. They screened the junkyard beyond the gates in which Mr. Penny scratched his living, just as his father and grandfather had done before him.

Joe crossed the pavement and paused at the gates. He never went to the front door. Neither did Mr. Penny, if he could help it. He lived mostly in the back of the house and only opened the front door for the postman, the milk-man, and the morning paper and, of course, anyone who called in a Rolls-Royce.

Joe lifted the latch and pushed the gate but it was badly warped and had dropped on its hinges. As the bottom board shuddered over the uneven cobbles the vibration shook the sign plate from its fastening. Joe picked it up and pressed it hard against the soft wood until the nails at either end were once more holding it in position. He stepped back then, eyeing it carefully, satisfying himself that the little wooden plaque that announced Mr. Penny's name and trade was level. It was a piece of cedar, so weathered and worn it must have been put there by his grandfather.

J. J. Penny & Son, it read, and underneath: *Second-hand Dealers*.

Joe never knew what J. J. stood for. Neither did anyone else, it seemed. And Mr. Penny didn't have a son. He didn't have any children at all. He did have a wife once. Joe didn't know whether she'd died or gone off with another man. It happened before he came. But the way Mr. Penny spoke sometimes about the faithfulness of animals and unfaithfulness of humans, Joe wondered.

Mr. Penny himself was quite impressive. This, of course, may have been due to his Panama hat, for he was a little man. He was always careful with his appearance, never being without a collar and tie, although sometimes he wore a dark gray ready-made bow in place of the tie. If you ran across him on the street (without his donkey and cart, of course) you'd have been hard put to name his trade. You might take him for a foreign tourist perhaps, or a visitor from the country, but never a Londoner who earned his living handling junk. Somewhere back in the distant past his ancestors had come from some foreign sunny land and that might account for the Panama hat; but he would have told you himself that it was cool and shady in the sun, and in the darkest winter it reminded him that summer was only a season away. Joe thought that was as good a reason as any, and although he wasn't sure where Panama was, he thought it a nice name for a hat.

Mr. Penny did his own housework and took pride in his business. But his greatest pride of all was the garden at the back. At one time the ground had been hired out in individual plots for vegetable and flower cultivation—in his father's time. But the holders who'd rented the plots from the late Mr. Penny had long since become late themselves, and when Carter's built their warehouse on the other side, it became an island of waste ground. The gate that had opened into Fowler's Alley had been broken down and people used to pop in and dump their rubbish at night. The weeds and rubbish had grown so thick that it had looked like a poor extension of the junkyard.

But not now. And never again. In the time that Joe had known Mr. Penny a transformation had taken place that was little short of a miracle. Even the yard was spruced up as if the picture it presented must conform (as near as it was possible for a junkyard to conform to anything) to the scene beyond.

Not that you'd get much inkling if you stood in the yard. True, the old cobblestones were brushed clean, and Mr. Penny always kept the sheds that formed two sides of the yard well primed with creosote. The wired-in compound where most of the scrap was stored was no longer such an eyesore since a patched tarpaulin covered most of it, and the open-fronted shed with its old donkey collars and leather and brass harness trappings hanging from the walls gave the surroundings almost a rural air. But you'd still never guess what there was at the back.

You'd have to go to the little gate between the side of the house and the woodshed, or look through the back window in Smokey's stable, and then what you saw would probably take your breath away.

But the few who came into the yard seldom went so far. They went no farther than it took to drive a quick bargain for something they wanted to buy or sell. Even the regular customers hardly noticed the change, and scarcely anyone who passed down Sparrow Street could have told you what lay behind the billboards, apart from the junkyard, that is.

It was always a surprise to Joe how few people ever noticed things, even when they were looking at them. Mr. Penny once said that most folks couldn't see beyond the end of their noses, except when they poked them into other people's business. Not that he disliked most folks. It wasn't their fault if they couldn't see far, and if they were human it was natural they should be interested in other humans. But no matter how tolerant you were, you couldn't help being irritated by some of them sometimes.

Joe often marveled at Mr. Penny's patience with people. Only once had he seen him lose his temper. That was the time they were making the garden and some hooligan leaned over the fence from Fowler's Alley and grabbed an armful of wallflowers, roots and all. Mr. Penny lost control then, and because he couldn't catch the culprit he threw his Panama hat at him. Luckily it didn't go over the fence or he might have lost that, too. But, normally, he was not given to such outbursts, and was always careful with his hat. He never got upset with a customer, even when the customer got on his high horse and looked down his nose, or went red in the face and swore like a trooper. Mr. Penny was always calm and his mild voice and manner of speaking remained unruffled.

Joe put it down to the animals. You had to have patience if you were fond of animals. They acted mostly on their own instincts and not on your instructions. Especially donkeys. The trouble he'd had getting Smokey to go sometimes would have tried the patience of a saint. But it never seemed to exhaust the patience of Mr. Penny. Mind you, he had a way with him, for in the end Smokey always gave in.

Joe shut the gate and crossed the yard to the back door. Usually, when he arrived, he peeped into Smokey's stable and then went to the little gate between the house and the woodshed, for likely as not Mr. Penny would be somewhere in the garden. But this time Joe went straight to the back door. He was curious about the man in the Rolls-Royce, and he was sure Mr. Penny must be still inside giving thought to his wealthy visitor. But when Joe got inside he found him giving thought to a pot of tea.

Mr. Penny always had a pot of tea mid-morning on Saturdays. Not counting Sunday, it was the one day of the week that he didn't go out on his rounds. Nobody wanted to see you when they were quitting work at twelve, and there was plenty to do in the workshop or the yard and in the garden. So he stayed at home but, whatever he was doing outside, he always came in and made a pot of tea mid-morning.

"Sit down, Joe," Mr. Penny said, getting up himself. "You're just in time. Thought you'd be along any minute, and put another spoonful in." He put the teapot on the table, and Joe sat down, watching him as he took another cup and saucer from the sideboard.

It was a nice sideboard. Wide and tall, in oak that was so dark it was almost black. It had four deep shelves with little brass hooks, and two drawers and cupboards below. It stood against the white-washed wall of the kitchen, the dark wood softening the harsh whiteness of the wall, with blue willow-patterned plates and dishes standing on edge along the shelves. Mr. Penny never used the plates or dishes; they'd been handed down by his mother, and probably her mother before that. They were so old the pattern had blurred and the rims were chipped, but they gave a kind of delicate air to the room. Rather like the owner himself, Joe thought.

Mr. Penny was getting on in years (though not as old as the plates and dishes, of course), and his face was patterned with the hard experience of living. But there were no chips, only here and there a gentle line, and a soft twinkle in his blue eyes. He was slight of build, and looked as if a puff of wind might blow him over; but he was strong inside or how else could he have coped with the heavy manual work sometimes necessary to his trade?

He pushed the cup of tea across the shiny oilcloth that covered his kitchen table.

"How's Aunt Ethel?" he asked.

"She went to the hospital," Joe said.

"What is it then? Boy or girl?" Mr. Penny's eyes twinkled.

"No one knows. It 'asn't come yet."

Mr. Penny nodded. "Nature always takes her time."

"Yes," said Joe. "And Nature's given Liz the measles."

9 ❧

"Oh, dear." Mr. Penny's mild, unruffled voice became even more gentle when there was sympathy in it. "That's a pity—with your aunt in her condition."

"That's why she had to go to the hospital. The doctor said she shouldn't get near anyone with measles."

"Is it the German measles?"

"I don't know which measles it is. She's got a lot of spots."

"How are you managing then?"

"Mrs. Quinton, from next door, helps. But that's why I 'aven't been around. I'm out of school and running errands and—well, you know what."

"Of course." Mr. Penny nodded again. "I know what. Is there anything I can do then—like writing to your Uncle Bert or—?" He hesitated, not sure what else he could do that a woman like Mrs. Quinton couldn't do better.

Joe shook his head, smiling his gratitude.

"No, thanks, Mr. Penny. Liz is writing to Uncle Bert. You've got enough to do, seeing after everything here. Are the pets all right?" he added anxiously. "I couldn't get around to feed them."

"You know me, Joe." His eyes were twinkling again. "I'm as fond of those creatures out there as you are. I wouldn't let them go without."

"What about Tinker?"

"Growing up right well, he is. And as happy as the rest o' them." He glanced at the window. "You know you need never worry about them, any o' them, when you're away."

Joe smiled. He knew.

10

He put down his cup and went to the open window. It was a large window draped with frilly white curtains, and the view it framed made the kitchen the best room in the house. When you stood there, looking out with the scent of lilac coming in, you might have been right in the heart of the country. That's where Joe had often wished he was —in the country. But since that day long ago when he'd met Mr. Penny and their magic experiment had turned the wasteland into a garden sanctuary, it was as good as getting his wish. The wide open spaces beyond London's distant limits could wait in the future for Joe. For now all he'd wished for was in the present, behind Mr. Penny's junkyard.

"What did the man in the Rolls-Royce want?" Joe asked quietly.

Mr. Penny looked at Joe still looking out of the window.

"He wants to buy the place," he said.

· Chapter Two ·

Joe was of average height, a little on the thin side, with curly brown hair and a round, freckled face. He had deep brown eyes that Mr. Penny reckoned would stir any girl's heart and any mother's pride, but his clothes would have stirred only sympathy. Rough serge trousers that, as a last resort, had been double-seated, and a blue seaman's jersey with patched elbows which had obviously been cast off by someone twice his age.

He lived on the first floor of Palfrey Buildings with

Aunt Ethel and his sister Liz. His Uncle Bert lived there, too, when he was home; but mostly he lived at sea. He was a steward on a cargo ship that tramped its way into every port in the world, but somehow always seemed to miss London. Of course, sometimes Uncle Bert came home, from Bristol or Glasgow or Liverpool. But his absence was so long each time that even Aunt Ethel would say she'd forgotten what he looked like. So Joe didn't see much of his uncle, and as you couldn't talk to women all the time, he'd been grateful for Alfie.

Uncle Bert had brought Alfie home in his knapsack on one of his rare shore leaves. He always brought home presents for the family. Usually it was some exotic foreign material that Aunt Ethel and Liz could make into a dress or a tablecloth or curtains. For Joe it might be peppermint rock candy or a snakeskin belt, and once he'd even brought a native pipe from India, but he'd never brought anything live before. Not that Alfie had been foreign; he'd been picked up from a pet trader in a Liverpool market after Uncle Bert had been having farewell drinks with the crew.

Joe had really set his heart on a rabbit, but Uncle Bert had told him that it wasn't fair to keep one on its own—fair to the rabbit, that is; and if you had two they multiplied so quickly, you'd need a garden to run them in. It was different with a tortoise. A tortoise was so slow that, by the time it got around to wanting company, Joe would be grown up and wanting another kind of company himself. That's what Uncle Bert had said.

Joe had to admit that a tortoise was a slow mover, although that didn't mean it was slow in other things. But

13 ✂

whatever the tortoise thought about it, Joe was very pleased, and he made Alfie a hutch and a stand from some old orange boxes, and Alfie lived in it outside the front door on the first floor landing. Every Monday morning, before the rent man called, Joe had to take the whole contraption into his bedroom because you weren't allowed to have pets in Palfrey Buildings.

It was all right to have babies there, or the measles, or to clean up the mess left on the outside landings by the pigeons, but you couldn't keep an animal on the premises. Mind you, some tenants did. Mrs. Isaacs, for instance. Everyone knew she kept a big ginger tom who kicked up a terrible din after dark, and old Mr. Sullavan had a very rude parrot, and Larry Barker, who went in for racing, often brought home a greyhound for the night; but nobody ever said anything. He supposed they didn't like the rent man.

Joe was very fond of animals. He'd go a long way out of his way just to see one, and was forever lingering around the livestock man in Pease Row market. The man always had his booth between the flower stall and the vegetable and fruit stand, which was more like the animals' natural surroundings than the jellied eels and the shoe and bootlace stalls opposite. But looking at the animals in their straw-lined cages only made it worse. It made you think of all the pictures in the books in the public library; the green fields, the waving corn, the streams and woods, peopled with so many small furry creatures that not even London Zoo could hold them all. If you stood there long enough watching the guinea pigs and rabbits, the puppies and the hens, you could almost forget you were in Pease

Row market until someone shouted at you to mind your back and you made way for a lumbering wheelbarrow. Then you stopped looking and thinking, and started walking, and that was your dream for the day.

And what good did it do? Nobody else understood. That's what Joe always thought. Until he met Mr. Penny.

It was funny really, in some ways—meeting Mr. Penny. Although the junkman had been in Sparrow Street all that time, with only Angel Square, Juke's Timber Yard, and the canal between him and Palfrey Buildings, Joe had never heard of the man before. Not that he would have thought much about him if he had. There was nothing special about dealers in scrap and junk. London was full of them, and Greenham borough in particular. So it was a lucky day for Joe when they happened to come together in Hope Street.

Early morning, it was, when he was delivering the newspapers. He'd seen the open cart with its yellow-spoked wheels outside the builder's yard, and the donkey standing very still between the bright red shafts. He'd seen Mr. Penny (although, of course, he didn't know it was Mr. Penny then) come out, carrying a broken lavatory cistern in one hand and some metal tubing in the other. He'd watched him place these carefully among the heap of odds and ends in the back, then climb onto the seat and take the reins. And just when Joe thought they were going to move off, the donkey fell down.

Joe was so surprised he dropped the newspapers in the gutter. He'd heard about donkeys that wouldn't go, and he'd been watching to see if this one would, but he'd never

15 ✂

expected it to fall down. For a moment he was so shocked he could do nothing. He thought the donkey was dead—until he saw the ears flick to and fro. Then he ran across the street to see if he could help.

"Is he all right?" Joe asked.

Mr. Penny was leaning over talking quietly to the animal. He straightened up when Joe spoke, and pushed his Panama hat to the back of his head.

"He will be. He gets a bit o' the rheumatics at times in his left foreleg. It makes him more stubborn than usual." He took a sugar cube from his pocket and showed it to the donkey. That seemed to do the trick. As soon as he tasted the cube he began to get up, assisted very gently by Mr. Penny. Joe helped, too, lifting a shaft to ease the burden as the donkey rose, and very soon he was standing easy on four legs, his tail swishing the dust of the street from his hindquarters.

Joe moved around, his hand stroking the warm, shaggy coat. He stopped at the front, caressing the animal's head, his fingers combing the tuft of hair between the tall ears.

"He's a nice fella," Joe said. "What's his name?"

"Smokey." Mr. Penny climbed up onto the cart and smiled down at him. "What's yours?"

"Joe."

"Well, thanks, Joe," he said warmly.

The boy stood back as the man took up the reins. He suddenly noticed the little brass sign above the front wheel. *J. J. Penny & Son*, it read. *Sparrow Street, E.*

"Can I come round and see 'ow Smokey is Saturday?" Joe asked.

The donkey turned and seemed to nod his head.

Mr. Penny leaned down in a kind of confidential way.

"Any friend of Smokey's is a friend o' mine, Joe," he said. "He's taken quite a fancy to you."

The cart moved forward, jerkily at first.

Joe waved.

"See you Saturday, then," he said.

And that had been the beginning. Every beginning must have an end, but who'd ever believe the end might come with a man in a Rolls-Royce?

· Chapter Three ·

The silence and the stillness seemed to last a long time. A lifetime. Yet it was really only seconds. Joe turned from the window to find that in those brief moments the world had changed.

The sun was still shining, the scent of lilac and tea leaves still hung in the kitchen air, but the room was different somehow. The tall sideboard, the willow-patterned plates, the long table topped with oilcloth were as homely and familiar as the shiny black grate and the broom cupboard door with the peg where Mr. Penny always hung his Panama hat. But there was something there that had never been there before. A shadow, perhaps. The shadow of the man in the Rolls-Royce.

"What would a man like that want with a place like this?" Joe wanted to know.

Mr. Penny stirred his second cup of tea.

"He wants to root it out," he said. His voice was calm, but his hand with the spoon in it trembled a bit.

"What d'you mean?"

"You know what happens, Joe, when you take a thing out by the roots. It's the end of that thing."

"You mean he wants to take away the house and the yard and—and—everything?"

"Everything," Mr. Penny said.

"But what for?"

"Money," Mr. Penny said sadly.

"But that's not a good enough reason to do such a thing."

"It's the only reason people like Mr. Massiter do anything."

Joe stared anxiously at the old man.

"But *you* wouldn't do it?" The words trembled over his lips. "You—you wouldn't sell the place?"

"No."

Joe sighed and the tension drained, leaving his shoulders sagging with relief.

"Well, that settles it," he said.

"It's not quite as easy as that, Joe. Big people, powerful people, don't take no for an answer." Mr. Penny pushed back his chair and went to the sideboard. At the back, under the lowest shelf, was a dark mahogany tea chest with an ivory lid. It must have held pounds of tea in its day; but now it only held Mr. Penny's domestic bills and receipts and his private and more important correspondence. He placed the chest on the table.

"Sit down, Joe," he said, going to the mantelpiece for his spectacle case.

Joe sat down, folding his arms. Mr. Penny sat opposite, pushing away his cup and saucer and drawing the tea chest in front of him. He took his glasses from the case and lodged them carefully over the bridge of his nose. They were very old glasses, gold-rimmed, without any frame or side support. They were clipped on with the aid of two tiny springs, and left little marks on the skin when he took them off. Whenever he wore them he always reminded Joe of an elderly schoolmaster, about to find fault with the exam papers. The lenses usually magnified the twinkle in his eyes, but this time the twinkle was hard to see.

"Listen, Joe," he said. "London's getting a new face. You've noticed that. Changes are going on all over the place. Buildings that were tumbled in the blitz have been cleared away and new ones put up in their place. The old ones left are being knocked down to fit in with the city's new plans. Like some of the other boroughs, Greenham is ripe for development and its turn is fast a-coming. Some call it progress, and in many ways I s'pose it is, but in the process some of the nice things get rooted out with the bad. That's what's gonna happen in Greenham, don't you see?"

Joe shook his head. He couldn't see.

"But they can't root out anything that belongs to you, specially if it's good, and if you don't want to sell." Joe's anguished look went through Mr. Penny's calm exterior and increased the hidden pain in his heart.

"Yes, they can, Joe. If it gets in the way."

"But that's not right."

"Anything the council or the government do is right." Mr. Penny sighed. It wasn't an apathetic sigh; it was more a reaction to the innocence and inexperience of youth.

"But it's got nothing to do with the council or the government, has it? I thought it was because of this—this fella in the Rolls Royce?"

Mr. Penny lifted the lid of the chest and began fumbling with some of the papers.

"Mr. Massiter is what they call a private interest," he said. "He owns land and buildings all over London."

"Well, then, he's got enough without this place, surely?"

"People never have enough, Joe, whatever they've got. But he's not the only one interested." Mr. Penny shook out a square of paper from the cluster in his hand. "Here's a letter from a real estate agent in the city." He fingered another. "This one's from a big builder in Paddington." He pushed the papers together. "There's another one from an investment company."

Joe couldn't believe it.

"D'you mean they're all wanting to buy the place?" he asked.

"That's what they're leading up to," Mr. Penny said.

"Well! They've got some cheek, I reckon. What do they take you for? Fancy trying to turn you out of your

21 ❧

own home just like that!"

"They make a big show about compensation."

"Compensation? How d'you mean?"

"Money. They'd pay a lot."

"What's the good of that if you lose the only thing you want?" Joe got up and thrust his hands into his pockets. He stood there, his shoulders hunched, his mind confused. He couldn't imagine Sparrow Street without Mr. Penny's house and the junkyard and their garden behind it.

"I know that, Joe." Mr. Penny was nodding his head in agreement. "Money's only paper and metal. It can buy more paper and metal and brick and mortar and the earth you stand on, but it can't buy the feeling you have for a place."

"O' course it can't." Joe leaned on the table. "So there's nothing to worry about, is there?"

Mr. Penny was silent for a moment. He shuffled the letters together and laid them on the table. Then he leaned back in his chair, took off his glasses, breathed on the lenses and rubbed them gently with his handkerchief. It was a slow, patient, unruffled movement, just like Mr. Penny's manner.

"You see, Joe," he said at last, "it's not just these big business fellas." He poked a finger at the letters. "It's these newfangled town-planning laws. They're the things what gets you in a muddle. You can't do this and you can't do that, not even on your own property. But some official can do it and even take your property away altogether if it spoils the plan." He finished polishing his glasses and put them back into the case.

"So what's gonna happen then?"

The old man looked up. A hard gleam of determination had replaced the soft twinkle in his eyes.

"Nobody seems to know for sure yet. But nothing's gonna happen to us here, if I can help it." He tapped the papers on the table. "I've taken no notice of these, but after the first arrived I went to see Mr. Hawkins, the borough surveyor. He told me there's gonna be changes in Sparrow Street."

"What changes?"

"Nothing said for certain, but I got a few hints, you might say. But there are obvious ones."

"Go on," said Joe.

"Well, for instance, I reckon the old factory's coming down across the road. And the trolley depot. The street'll be wider, that's for sure. Whatever's done, you can bet a cat's whisker that I'll lose the billboards. So there'll be no more rent from the posters when they come down."

"So what are they gonna do when they've knocked everything down?"

"Put something else up. They have plans, my lad. New modern buildings. Some'll be shops most likely, others offices and maybe flats. But Mr. Hawkins says as how I shouldn't do anything hasty. About the letters, that is. He says it might be best to leave things alone for a bit. He was very friendly. He knows this is my living; but he thinks the way things may turn out I might be wise to think about any private offer."

"What does he think that for?" Joe couldn't get to the bottom of it.

"He doesn't say. None o' them officials ever do. But you see, Joe, if the council plans to make this a smart, new street, you can reckon they won't want my yard in it."

Joe sat down again, his brows drawing together so that his naturally open face closed in a dark scowl.

"I'd like to tell this Mr.—er—What's-'is-Name—this borough fella . . .?"

"Mr. Hawkins?"

"That's him. I'd like to tell him all we done on this place," Joe said with feeling.

"He knows. He understands. He's very sorry, but it's progress, Joe." Mr. Penny sighed. It was painful growing up. Learning sums and history dates was easy compared with learning about life. There was no friendly teacher to soften the blows or help you over the obstacles. You had to learn the hard way. By experience. And one of the first things you learned was that nothing was permanent—not even happiness.

"So you see how it is, laddie," Mr. Penny went on. "Things have to change. All things."

Joe watched him push the papers back into the tea chest. Mr. Penny was a good man. He minded his own business. He was fond of animals. He wouldn't lift a finger or utter a word that might harm a soul. It didn't seem right that all he'd worked for, all he had feeling for, might be rooted out and swept away on account of progress. Out of nothing they'd made their garden. A tiny scrap of green amidst the gray. Whatever they knocked down or put up on Sparrow Street, surely they could leave such a small piece of it alone? It wasn't much to ask. So why didn't *he* start by asking Mr. Hawkins?

"P'raps if *I* went to see Mr. Hawkins, I could . . ." The words seemed to collide in Joe's throat and all sounds ceased as Mr. Penny turned halfway between the table and the sideboard. There was a reproving look on his face as he put the open chest back on the table.

"It wouldn't do a scrap o' good," he said, and the gentle tone of his voice took the little bit of severity out of his look. "I tell you, my lad, it's not just the council, it's them private interests as well." He glanced down at the papers crammed into the chest. "They've a lot o' influence. They're the ones that have the money to buy and build. They make their plans fit in with the council's redevelopment schemes. They work in with the officials, don't you see?"

Joe nodded. He was beginning to see.

"It's mostly the private money what puts up the commercial places," Mr. Penny went on. "The public money —that is, what the council spends—looks after the roads and the drains and the trash cans and things like that."

"So these private people are the ones, then?"

"Well, yes, in a manner o' speaking." Mr. Penny fingered the lid of the chest. "Soon as they get to hear an area is to be developed, they get in and buy the best sites. Like Mr. Massiter. He's bought Carter's warehouse."

"He's bought that, too!" Joe was taken aback.

Mr. Penny nodded. "You see why he's so interested in this place that he comes down here himself. He wants to extend right across and have a frontage on Sparrow Street."

"What—right across the garden!" Joe said in horror.

"What else?" Mr. Penny spread out his hands helplessly. "That's why he's more anxious than anyone else. First there was this letter and then on Thursday some

25 ❧

legal fella arrives from the company giving me a lot o' rigmarole. He was a starchy one, he was, and so clever you'd never believe it. I couldn't understand half he said, so he didn't get much answer out o' me. Then this morning the Big Chief himself arrives."

"To try and make you sell?" Joe's eyes were a somber black.

"O' course. He's so scared someone else might step in. Now he's got the warehouse he doesn't want to lose the site that'll give him frontage on Sparrow Street."

"Well, go on," said Joe in a dull voice. "What did he say?"

"Oh, a whole lot o' things. He's very polite, you see. Says he wanted to make me acquaintance; he didn't want any misunderstandings or bad feelings, that's why he'd come himself in person. Says he knew my difficulties, it being my home and business, but he thought I should consider what he could offer—more than enough to keep me in luxury for the rest o' my life. Somewhere else, o' course." Mr. Penny gestured with his hands again. "I ask you, Joe, don't that make you think? He pays all that money just to get me out and knock the place down. So you can reckon he'll get a fortune for what he puts up."

"What did you tell him, then?"

"That money made no difference to me. I'd always had enough for my wants, and as for luxury—well, luxury for me was living the way I want to live, which is what I been doing all my life."

Joe nodded. He understood.

"So you told him about—us, and the garden and the animals, and how we started it all?" he suggested.

"I told him, Joe," Mr. Penny said quietly. "But he didn't seem very interested. He glanced out o' the window once but I reckon all he could see was money."

"Well, what happened in the end? How did you leave things?"

"Oh, still in the air a bit. I says as how I wouldn't do anything hasty, and he agrees. He says he understands I'd need to consider the offer. Any help and advice he could give me about the council and lawyers, I had only to ask. But under all the soft talk and the polite manners, I could see he means business. He's a hard, determined man, Joe, who's always got what he wants and to hell with the consequences. But I'm not giving in. I'm not leaving Sparrow Street till I'm driven out." Mr. Penny closed the tea chest, and his eyes were moist, but whether because of the sad thought of being driven out or because of the strain of reading all those letters, Joe didn't know.

Something had to be done. They couldn't just let things happen. They were responsible not just for themselves and the house and business, but for the garden and the innocent creatures who lived in it. He must think of something. Something bold and determined, like they did in movies. But he couldn't think of anything at the moment.

Mr. Penny returned the tea chest to the sideboard and put on his Panama hat. He crossed over and tapped Joe affectionately on the shoulder.

"Come on, me lad," he said. "Let's take a look in the garden and forget about people and money. It's time you fed our friends outside. You'd never believe how they've missed you, Joe." He opened the back door and stepped into a shaft of light that was thick with sunbeams. They seemed to form a circle close to the crown of the Panama hat, and brought a kind of glow to the figure on the doorstep. It made a bright picture, but sunbeams were only specks of dust, which was what everything came to in the end. But that was in the end. And this was only the beginning and already the dearest things they had were threatened.

It was then that Joe saw the little white card under the table. It must have fallen from the tea chest when Mr. Penny had pulled out the papers. He picked it up and read the neat engraving: *Mr. Arnold Massiter, 7 Eleigh Place, Regent's Park, N.W.1.*

He put it on the table, then all in a second, changed his mind. When he joined Mr. Penny outside he was fingering the card in his pocket. Together they went through the little gate between the house and the woodshed and into the garden. Mr. Penny began walking and pointing and talking, but Joe didn't take much notice. He was wondering how far it was to Regent's Park.

· Chapter Four ·

It isn't an easy journey from Greenham borough to Regent's Park—especially when you haven't got enough for the bus fare. And Joe hadn't. Not there *and* back, anyway. To make it more difficult, Tinker was getting restless in his traveling box. Joe began to wonder if the whole expedition was going to be worth it. But once you start a thing you shouldn't turn back.

He'd made up his mind to see Mr. Massiter. He had to show him just what his money and the council's plans would do to an old man like Mr. Penny. He had to show him just what they were trying to take away.

That's where Tinker, his pet weasel, came in. He represented the animals who lived in Mr. Penny's garden. Joe represented Mr. Penny. Sometimes it was much better to speak up for someone than for the person to speak for himself. Especially a person like Mr. Penny who, in the unexpected interview on Saturday morning, had probably left a lot unsaid. Joe and Tinker might bring home to Mr. Massiter the real picture he should have seen (instead of the money) when he looked out of the kitchen window.

Joe would have to explain, of course. Tell the story from the beginning. How they'd started the garden, how the pets had grown from one tortoise and the hedgehog through the guinea pigs and rabbits and the gray squirrel right up to their youngest and latest playmate, Tinker. And that was without counting Smokey, and the two stray cats, and the birds who found the garden a quiet mating place. Then there was the other side of the picture: Mr. Penny's living, his home, his feeling for the place he'd lived in all his life. Everything that made his existence (and Joe's) worthwhile was on Sparrow Street. No one—not even one as hard as Mr. Penny said Mr. Arnold Massiter was—could fail to see the wrong of taking away something that was so right.

Of course, Mr. Penny didn't know—about the journey to Regent's Park, that is. He'd have had a blue fit if he'd known what was in Joe's mind. But Joe had told no one what was in his mind. He'd made his plan secretly, over the weekend. Not that it had been the sort of weekend in which you could make plans easily, secret or otherwise. What with Mrs. Quinton popping in from next door and giving him errands to run, Liz taking advantage of her measles to get him to do jobs in the flat, and Aunt Ethel having the baby, it was hard to put your mind to anything serious at all. But Joe managed. All the time—even when he went to the hospital with a bunch of flowers and Mrs. Quinton on Sunday afternoon—he was deciding what to do about Mr. Massiter. In fact, going to the hospital had been reassuring in one way. The scene in the maternity ward seemed to confirm the soundness of his intention of taking Tinker with him to Regent's Park.

After he'd given Aunt Ethel the bunch of flowers Mr. Penny had sent with his congratulations, Joe had stood back near the foot of the bed while Mrs. Quinton made a fuss over the new boy. She beamed and cooed and seemed so full of love and kindness that it was difficult to believe she could be the same person who had looked so harsh and cheerless in her black apron and curlers a few hours before. Joe thought Mrs. Quinton wasn't the only one who could look harsh and cheerless first thing in the morning. Probably most of the other visitors in the ward could look the same, but now they glowed with a pride and affection that filled the clinical atmosphere of the place with warmth.

Small, helpless things seemed to bring out the best in people. Mightn't a small, helpless creature like Tinker do just that for Mr. Massiter? Joe reckoned it might.

So it had been settled. Monday was the day. And just about noon, after Mr. Penny had gone off on his rounds,

31 ❦

Joe had slipped over to Sparrow Street. He'd taken Tinker from his spacious run and gently placed him in the grass-lined traveling box, and with a small bottle of water and some scraps of meat in his pockets, he'd set off for Regent's Park.

It was when he boarded the bus at Mile End Road that Tinker began to get restless. Up till then the little creature had been so quiet that Joe had raised the hinged flap a couple of times to reassure himself that all was well. But Tinker had gone to sleep and had slept through the alley and the back street walk which had taken them to White-cross Gate. In fact, he remained so quiet that even the inspector at the bus stop at Mile End Road wasn't aware of Joe's traveling companion when Joe asked him the cheapest way to Regent's Park.

The inspector put him on a Number Twenty-five and told him to get off at Oxford Circus and walk up Regent Street past Broadcasting House and ask about Eleigh Place when he reached Park Crescent. Joe said he'd do that. But on the top deck of the bus, all the jolting and the stopping and the starting and the noise upset Tinker so much that Joe thought they'd have to get off before they got to the city.

It didn't come to that. He thrust the thought of failure from his mind and tried to tempt Tinker with some of the meat scraps. They did the trick. The shy creature forgot his anxiety when he scented the food.

Joe was tipping the last of the scraps from the paper bag into the traveling box when the conductress came up for the fares. He quickly emptied the bag, closed the flap of the box, and placed it close beside him on the seat where it was screened by his jacket. He was afraid she might charge him another fare if she saw he wasn't alone, but he needn't have worried. She didn't notice anything. She had soft blue eyes and a diamond ring on her finger. She was feeling generous with the world. And what nice girl wouldn't when she was getting married on Saturday. She called him *love* and only charged him sixpence, and when she put him off at Oxford Circus she told him which way to go, and to mind the road and wished him luck, although he knew she couldn't know what his errand was. Still, her friendly manner cheered him up no end and he'd certainly been lucky over the fare. Maybe that was a good omen for his forthcoming interview.

He was feeling much better now, more confident about seeing things through. Tinker had settled down again, so he must have been feeling better, too. Finding Park Crescent was easy and there he asked a postman the way to Eleigh Place. After a lot of lefts and rights and crossings-over, he came at last to a wide, short, tree-lined road with a low wall and dense trees at the end of it.

Eleigh Place was very quiet, with large, white-fronted stone houses that stood in their own spacious grounds protected by trees. He walked a little way down and stopped under a sycamore to take a look around and realized he was right outside Number Seven.

The figure was painted on the huge, white, square pillars at either side of the gateway. The gates were open and the wide gravel drive disappeared beneath a canopy of ash trees. But through the foliage you could just make out the blank whiteness of the house, and here and there the glint of sunlight reflecting on windows.

Joe stood there waiting, watching, wondering; but there was no one to see. No sound or movement except, in the background, the distant roar of London's traffic. He pushed the crumpled visiting card back into his pocket, stepped toward the gateway, and paused again. Suddenly, he placed Tinker's box on the low wall of the garden of Number Seven, carefully raised the flap, and gently stroked the small, brown furry head inside.

He leaned over the box, his mouth so close to the open flap that his breath ruffled the animal's fur.

"It's you and me, Tinker," Joe said softly. "You and me against the Big Man, so just you behave."

Tinker moved his head up and down as if he understood the implications. His long whiskers tickled Joe's chin, and as his nose caught the scent of the nearby vegetation he started to raise himself to look around. Joe quickly pushed him back, dropped the flap and turned the little wooden button that kept it in place. Then he walked up the drive.

A couple of sparrows made a fuss as he passed their hedge, and a blackbird screeched an alarm from a sprawling rhododendron shrub, but no one appeared at the house when it came in view.

It was a big place, with tall windows on either side of the front door. The door was all white and made of large panels, and sheltered by a stone porch topped by a balcony. The drive skirted the edge of a lawn and then divided. One arm swept around to the steps leading up to the porch, the other passed alongside the house, then curved away into a cluster of trees.

Joe moved hesitantly toward the steps. The place was

so grand and he felt so small that he was sure no one would see him even if they were looking. But he wasn't so confident now. It was a bit overwhelming.

He went carefully up the steps and stood before the great front door until his knees stopped wobbling. He had that strange, sickly feeling inside that he always got when he had to see the school dentist. The hesitation and the inactivity seemed to make it worse, so he made the effort and jabbed the bell.

It was funny how quickly the feeling went away when the door opened, even though the man who stood there wasn't Mr. Massiter and couldn't have looked more unwelcoming. He was tall and thin with a bit of dark hair smoothed down on top, and raised eyebrows. He was dressed in a dark suit with a long tail coat and a black tie. He looked down from a great height and, to add to it, the doorway was another step up from the porch. But he had the kind of look that made you feel you were a long way down, anyway.

"I've come to see Mr. Massiter," Joe said. "Mr. Arnold Massiter."

The eyebrows went even higher.

"Mr. Massiter is not here." He spoke in a severe, clipped voice, and suddenly looked so stiff and starchy he didn't seem real. "And he never sees anyone without an appointment."

"Well, he called on Mr. Penny without an appointment," Joe said.

"I know nothing of Mr. Massiter's activities outside his private residence." He glanced distastefully down at Joe, noticing the unusual, boxlike object in the boy's hand.

"If you're selling anything, I'll tell you now we never buy at the door." And he began to close it.

"Just a minute, mister," said Joe. "I'm not selling anything. I've come all the way from Greenham to see Mr. Massiter about Mr. Penny's house and the garden and all our animals in Sparrow Street. Mr. Massiter wants . . ."

The man raised a bony hand and Joe stopped talking.

"No point at all in telling me." He took a deep breath through his nose which made his nostrils quiver as if he was sniffing a bad smell, but he couldn't smell anything really. It was only that he was getting concerned because he didn't know what the boy was talking about but was sure his presence was a cover for some ulterior motive. "I don't want to waste your time," he went on briskly, "or my time or Mr. Massiter's time, so my advice to you is to go back to wherever you came from and write a letter. Understand? Write a letter stating your business. No doubt, then, an appointment will be arranged."

"Got no time for letter writing. This is urgent."

"And what I'm telling you is final." He bent slightly toward Joe, which was a very difficult thing for such a stiff person to do. "You can take or leave my advice, as you wish, but I am ordering you off these premises now."

"I'm not taking orders or advice from you," Joe blurted out, incensed by the high-handed manner. "I came all this way to see Mr. Massiter and I'm sure *he'll* want to see *me*. So I'm gonna wait here till he comes." He felt the color flooding his cheeks as he realized how rude his anger had made him.

The color was flooding the lean face of the man at the door, too. Ordinarily, he was as urbane and aloof and unruffled as most butlers appear to be, but his day so far had been rather out of the ordinary and this final straw was beginning to throw him off balance. What with the cook giving notice, and the embarrassing moments that morning when he was caught in the crossfire of an argument between the master and madam, it was enough to curdle the edge of even the calmest nerves. And now, at any time at all, the master would be back for his overnight bag and there was still his stomach powder and his throat lozenges to find, and here he was wasting time politely trying to shoo away this brazen urchin from somewhere in the East End. He could just imagine how the master would react if he found the boy awaiting him, whatever the reason might be, when he was hurrying to get the flight to Amsterdam.

Joe, of course, was not aware of all this, but he could see that his defiance had made the man angry. He couldn't help it. He hadn't come all this way with Tinker to be put off his objective by a servant. Under the anger and the frustration he was near to tears.

"If you don't mind, I'll wait," he said a little more respectfully.

"I've told you, you won't see Mr. Massiter without an appointment, and you certainly won't see him today." Joe stepped back and leaned against one of the pillars of the porch.

"I'll wait," he said. "And we'll hear what Mr. Massiter says about that."

"You'll do no such thing here." The color in the lean face was turning a faint shade of blue. Suddenly he came out of the house and, acting in a way far beneath the dignity of his calling, he took Joe by the scruff of the neck and marched him down the steps.

Joe struggled frantically in the bony grip as they staggered across the drive. In the confusion he somehow managed to worm his foot between his assailant's ankles and the next moment they were both sprawling in a rhododendron bush. Tinker's box fell from Joe's grasp, and as it slid through the green stems the button over the flap was torn away. Before Joe could recover, Tinker's head had pushed up the little hatch and at panic-stricken speed his long, brown body glided out of the box and rapidly disappeared across the garden.

To add to the confusion, at the same moment a large, dark, chauffeur-driven car swung in through the gates and came to a silent stop beside them.

· Chapter Five ·

At first Joe thought the car was the black Rolls-Royce
and that Mr. Massiter would step out and angrily demand
to know what was going on, but it was a dark blue Mercédès and before the chauffeur could jump to the rear
door, it opened and a woman appeared.

Joe was too concerned for Tinker to take any further
notice. He picked up himself and the empty traveling box,
turned his back on the company, and started to move
around the rhododendron bush. But the man, who was

trying to regain his dignity, suddenly grabbed his arm and pulled him back.

"Parker—whatever trouble is this? What's happened?" The woman spoke in a firm voice, but it was a quiet firmness and there was a kind light in her large dark eyes, especially when she looked at Joe, who began wriggling in the man's grasp.

"Let me go!" It was a demand, not a plea.

But Parker held on to him with one hand while awkwardly trying to brush the dust from his previously immaculate suit with the other. He cleared his throat. "Begging your pardon, madam. I can't rightly say what this grubby urchin's objective is in coming here and demanding to see the master, but he insisted on loitering on the premises. I objected to his obstreperous manner and was escorting him to the gate when he tripped me . . ."

"You fell over your own big feet!" Joe said. "Let go!" He twisted right around until he was facing the woman and the chauffeur again, but he couldn't get free.

The woman nodded.

"Let him go, Parker," she said.

"Very well, madam." The grip relaxed and Joe stepped to one side. He was going to dive off into the garden but the woman was looking at him and he hesitated.

"What's your name?" she asked.

"Joe." Still he hesitated. She was smiling now, and the contrast between her smile and the stony faces of Parker and the chauffeur was clear enough to suggest that he could count on her as a friend.

"Well, Joe, perhaps you'd like to tell us about it."

"When I've found Tinker I will." The statement was

defiant but the defiance was lost in the urgency of his voice. "Look!" He held up the empty traveling box. "The catch broke off when we fell down. He got out." He glanced toward the profusely stocked garden. "He'll get lost in there. . . . He's not used to it."

"Who's Tinker?" asked the woman.

"My weasel," Joe said.

"Is *that* what it was in there?" Parker was looking down his nose at the box. "I thought the boy was trying to sell something."

"Weasel?" muttered the chauffeur. "Aren't they dangerous?"

"Might be if you cornered one." Joe suddenly noticed that the chauffeur was not the dark-suited driver he'd seen in Mr. Massiter's Rolls-Royce in Sparrow Street on Saturday morning. But the revelation only added to the confusion so he forgot it and went on, "Tinker's not dangerous. He's tame. He's not very old and he's scared stiff with all this fuss and he'll lose himself in the garden. . . ." The words tumbled out and Joe started to move away, but again the woman stopped him.

"A weasel seems an unusual pet—to take around, anyway," she said. "You're not trying to sell him?"

"Oh, no," Joe said. "He's one of my animals from Sparrow Street. I just brought him along to show Mr. Massiter. I said I'd tell you—but I have to find him first." There was a look of anguish on his freckled face.

"All right, Joe," the woman said quietly. "I'm Mrs. Massiter. We'll all help to find him. He won't be able to get out of the garden; it's surrounded by a high wall."

"You don't know weasels," Joe said, moving off. "This

41 ✄

is the way he went, I'm sure."

Mrs. Massiter turned to her chauffeur. "Lawton—will you go down and warn the gardener?"

"Warn him, ma'am?"

"Don't quibble, Lawton. You know what I mean. Tell him there's a weasel running loose."

Lawton touched his cap.

"Yes, ma'am." He looked at Parker. "Where is he?"

"How should I know?" Parker said testily, and nodded after Joe. "He must have gone that way."

"I don't mean the weasel. I mean Hoskins."

"He was doing something in the rock garden this morning." Parker began to brush the remaining specks of dust from the tails of his coat. You could see he wasn't very pleased with the way things were going and was dreading the sudden arrival of the master.

"You and Hoskins come up slowly from the lower garden," Mrs. Massiter instructed Lawton. "Parker, Joe, and I will make a search down toward you." She turned and went off, following Joe.

"Yes, ma'am. A kind of frontal sweep." Lawton had been in the army and wished he was still there. He'd been a chauffeur to a major-general and no doubt because of it he tried to interpret every little operation in military terms. Driving a major-general was nice and steady and precise; driving a woman was not like that at all. They were so emotional, which made them unpredictable, which made for a very unsettled existence. Particularly with a woman like Mrs. Massiter who was fond of animals and children and had neither. You never knew what you'd be asked to do next—like this hunt in the garden, for instance. Looking for a weasel—even if you knew what it looked like—was like looking for the proverbial needle in the haystack. Still, orders were orders. And the sight of Parker, forced from his high-falutin' perch in the household to grovel in the garden, more than made up for every disadvantage Lawton found in his job. It was moments like these you'd miss, driving a major-general. He grinned across at the butler.

"If we had more troops we could fan out," he said. "What about calling up Daisy and Cook?"

Parker was lifting the legs of his trousers to protect the bottoms from the dirt as he delicately stepped across a flower bed.

"Oh, get on, Lawton," he said impatiently. "We're not playing soldiers. The sooner we find this wretched animal and remove it and the boy from the premises, the better."

Lawton was right. It was a bit like a military operation. There was a certain amount of precision about it, although this was probably due to the meticulous manner in which Parker maneuvered himself through the shrubs and trees to avoid sustaining a mark on his polished shoes or a tear in his clothing. It was strange country to him. He'd never ventured off the drive or beyond the terrace before.

It was strange to Joe, too. He was very impressed with the vastness of the garden and the neat density of its shrubbery. He didn't know anything about the military aspect. He'd never had the opportunity to play with soldiers. He might have been pleased if he'd realized how he'd taken command of the situation, but he was too anxious about Tinker to notice.

43 ❦

"What does a weasel look like?" Mrs. Massiter, moving stealthily, closed in on Joe. "I don't think I've ever seen one."

"Long body," whispered Joe, peering ahead. "Small, sort of pointed face, brown fur all over his back, white belly—" He broke off, stopped and pointed. "There he is now!"

They had passed the garage which stood, partially concealed by trees, on one side of the house, and were creeping down a gently sloping path shaded by young sycamores, birch, and hazel, when Tinker appeared around the slim trunk of a beech tree.

"He's quite pretty," murmured Mrs. Massiter. "But he looks a little ferocious."

"Ssh!" whispered Joe. "He might be after a squirrel." He held up his hand as Parker joined them. "Ssh! Keep back. Don't make a noise." He began to creep forward on his own.

It would probably have been all right if Parker hadn't sneezed. A floating feather dropped by a startled bullfinch grazed the tip of his nose, and he was too slow to stifle the ensuing gust. In the stillness it sounded like a minor explosion to Joe. It must have sounded like that to Tinker as well, for he suddenly scampered to the ground and vanished in a clump of fern.

"I beg your pardon, madam," Parker apologized miserably, avoiding the cold stares of his companions. "Most unfortunate—I . . ."

"Keep your trap shut, mister, will you?" Joe interrupted softly. "He's on the ground now. Come on—quietly!"

They resumed the trail.

Tinker was no easy quarry. Whether he was really scared or actually got some kind of animal kick out of leading so many people on a chase, you couldn't tell. But there was no doubt that his dash for freedom was thawing some of the ice that formed a barrier between the social worlds of Eleigh Place and Sparrow Street.

Tinker would appear at intervals ahead of them as they followed him down toward the lower garden, but they never caught up with him. Joe called his name (and under his breath Parker called him a lot of other things); but it made no difference. The slinky brown body on the short furry legs had always disappeared again by the time they reached the spot where he had last shown himself.

The lower garden at the back of the house was a riot of color—greens and reds, yellows, mauves and scarlets. The flowers, shrubs, and trees formed a perfect setting for the white-walled house, with its stone-balustraded terrace stepping down to the close-cropped lawns and neat pathways. And it was on one of the twisting paths that they suddenly came face to face with Lawton. He held a finger to his lips.

"Hoskins is the other side of the hedge," he whispered. "He thought he saw something moving in the delphiniums."

A little farther down there was a gap in the shrubs. Joe led the way through, only to find that Hoskins was at the other end of a series of rustic arches which formed a rose walk. Joe ran down the walk and at the end found that the gardener had taken a paved path leading across to the lawn. Joe caught up with him halfway along.

45 ✂

"Where is he?"

Hoskins suddenly stopped, and began looking on one side of the path and then the other.

"Slippery customer that weasel o' yours," he said, tipping his battered hat and scratching some isolated gray hairs. "Seems to have gone agin now." Hoskins was an elderly man with a permanent stoop and a dry leathery face. He looked as if he'd been out in the garden all his life, and by the crick in his back he could have spent most of it weeding.

"You got close to him?" Joe said.

"Aye, he was on this path then cut off into the azaleas there. If we could flush him out and drive him just a bit farther, we'd have him on the lawn where we could see him."

"Have you lost him, Hoskins?" Mrs. Massiter had come up, flanked by Parker and Lawton.

"No, don't think so, ma'am." He touched his hat. "I was just saying to the boy here, if we can drive him ahead o' us to the lawn, we should pick him up easy."

Parker was mopping his brow and looked as if he was going to suggest that he be excused from further proceedings, but he suggested nothing for Mrs. Massiter said, "Well, let's do that, Hoskins." And that's what they did.

Forming a line abreast they moved through the garden rather like the beaters on a pheasant shoot, and before they reached the lawn Tinker appeared on it. Joe ran ahead, the others spread out wide on either side, and the sweep moved slowly across the grass. Tinker sensed the error of exposing himself and suddenly turned toward the cover of the rock garden, which sloped away at the farther edge of the lawn. Joe swung around to head him off, gesturing to the others to form a circle. A few moments later Tinker was surrounded. He crouched down on the grass and waited, and the advancing circle halted. As if calling reserves, Lawton beckoned to the maid and the cook, who had been drawn out onto the terrace by the strange capers on the lawn.

They came down the steps; Daisy, tall and thin, in a navy dress with a white lace apron, Mrs. Flowers, short, stoutish, in a long white coverall. They hurried across the lawn toward the circle that was now edging in on the crouching animal.

Joe suddenly noticed the newcomers' approach and held up his hand. Everybody stopped.

"Mustn't crowd him too much," he said softly. "He might have a fit."

No one heard what he said, but they remained in the background as he went forward, bending low and whispering encouraging endearments.

Tinker remained still, watching Joe. He was almost within touching distance. Everyone stood transfixed, trying to hold their breath. It was so quiet you could hear the plop of the fish in the rock-garden pool as they came up for the flies.

And then it happened. The spell and the stillness were shattered. A voice, it was—booming out from the terrace like distant gunfire. . . .

"*Par-ker!* . . . *PAR-KER!* . . . What's going on down there?"

Every pair of eyes flashed from Tinker to the terrace. Parker moved first. He bowed his way out from the

47 ✂

circle with a glance at Mrs. Massiter.

"If you'll excuse me, madam," he said tremulously. "The master will be wanting his overnight bag. . . ."

Joe reached down to grab Tinker but the opening made by Parker's sudden withdrawal was too much of a temptation. Tinker bolted across the lawn and down the rock-garden steps to the pool.

· Chapter Six ·

It couldn't have been a worse introduction. There was Joe, up to his waist in the ornamental pool, clutching a dripping weasel to his chest while terrified fish of silver and gold darted in all directions.

True, he'd caught Tinker before the little runaway had done any fatal damage, but Joe himself had knocked over a cherubic statue as he'd jumped into the water and now had the stem of a water lily wrapped around his thighs.

It was a fine state of affairs in which to come face to

face with Mr. Massiter, but it wasn't his fault. Parker was to blame. If he hadn't tried to march him off the premises as though he were a common thief, there would have been no struggle and Tinker would have had no chance to escape.

Parker had gone now. So had everyone else who'd joined the chase, except Mrs. Massiter. Even Hoskins had quietly vanished before the master came down the rock-garden steps to the pool.

Joe felt on his own and scared. Silly, too. Silly because he didn't know what to say and scared he'd do more damage if he moved. He just stood there, trying to take his eyes away from the thundery face of the man he'd seen leaving Mr. Penny's house on Saturday morning. But he couldn't. Take his eyes away, that is. It was as if his gaze and the steely stare of the man on the edge of the pool were locked in a kind of combat.

Mrs. Massiter was the first to break the tense silence. She stooped and picked up the traveling box which Joe had dropped at the side of the pool.

"Now you've caught him you'd better come out, Joe," she said. "You'll get nothing but a cold standing there."

He glanced from one to the other, then began to wade cautiously to the side.

Joe had expected an explosion when Mr. Massiter opened his mouth, but though the anger was there in the harshness of the voice, it was well under control.

"Perhaps someone would kindly tell me what's going on."

No one said anything and the man glanced sharply at the woman.

"Well, Laura? I couldn't get any sense out of Parker."

"I should have thought it was obvious," she said, reaching over and helping Joe from the pool.

"I'm asking you, Laura, for an explanation." He came closer. "I find your car in the drive, the house empty, and you and the staff frolicking about on the lawn like a lot of delinquents. Who's this boy—and that thing he's holding—and look at the shocking state of the pool!"

"There's a perfectly simple explanation, Arnold," she said. "Joe lost his weasel and we had to find the creature before he got out of the garden."

"Weasel? Is that what the thing is?"

"He's no *thing*, either." Joe suddenly found his voice. "He's alive and he's got feelings just like you or me or anyone else."

That brought a faint smile to the corners of Mrs. Massiter's nice mouth, but her husband's remained tight and unrelenting.

"How did they get into the garden in the first place?" he wanted to know.

"Joe came to see you," she said.

"See me?"

"Yes."

"What could he possibly want with me?"

"It don't seem much good now," Joe said.

There was a sound behind them, a faint clearing of the throat. They turned and found Parker on the steps.

"Begging your pardon, sir," he said. "Your secretary is on the telephone."

"I'll be there in a moment." Mr. Massiter waved him off impatiently.

"And if I might remind you, sir, of your time," Parker persisted gently with a distasteful glance at Joe and Tinker. "London Airport—five-thirty."

"What is it now?"

Parker consulted a gold pocket watch.

"Six and a half minutes past three." He looked up, his face now impassive. "Everything is ready, sir, including your bath."

Mr. Massiter nodded, dismissing Parker, and climbed the steps. At the top he paused, looking back.

"I can't think what the boy can want, but you can take care of him, Laura."

"That was my intention," she said.

Joe was relieved to see him go. He couldn't expect to get any change of heart out of him now, not after that scene. Mr. Penny was right. The man was hard, determined, and always got what he wanted. But he didn't look like that kind of man. Not close up. He had quite a pleasant face really, a bit mottled and fleshy but still good looking. His dark hair was beginning to gray at the temples, and he was slightly overweight but not really fat. But it was no use having good looks if you were bad underneath. And Joe thought he was.

Mrs. Massiter was different. She wasn't very tall, a bit on the thin side, and apart from her soft, brown eyes, she didn't have much in the way of good looks. But maybe all the good things about her were in her heart. That's what Joe reckoned as he watched her replace the little cherubic figure on its pedestal.

"Now," she said smiling, "the first thing is to get those wet clothes off. And you'd better take a nice, long hot shower so you don't catch cold."

"I'm all right, it's Tinker," Joe said. "He's really soaked. I can't put him in his box till he's dried off."

"We'll soon take care of that," she said. "We'll take him up to the potting shed. There are some sacks there. Hoskins can fix up a little bed on the bench in front of the window, and Tinker will dry in the sun."

On the way to the potting shed Joe began to talk. He talked about himself and Aunt Ethel and Uncle Bert and Liz and Palfrey Buildings, but most of all he talked about Mr. Penny and the garden and the home they'd made there for their animal friends. It was surprising how much you could say on a short walk when you had a good listener.

After leaving Tinker in Hoskins' care, they continued to the house, Joe resuming his story right up to the moment of Mr. Massiter's visit to Sparrow Street on Saturday morning. At that point he had to break off because they'd reached the cloakroom.

Well, that's what Mrs. Massiter called it. There was no sign of any cloaks. But there was a washbasin and a lavatory. The floor seemed to be a kind of cork, with mats on it, and the walls were green tiles. There were mirrors with lights and glass shelves and a stool and a radiator along one wall and a closet at one end. At the other end was a long door of crinkled glass that you couldn't see through.

Mrs. Massiter opened the door.

"This is the shower," she said.

It was like a large cupboard inside with a tiled floor that had a small drain in the center. Two small chromium levers in the wall worked the water jets fixed in the wall. On the door rail behind a waterproof curtain was a large white towel.

She pointed to the levers which he could now see were lettered *H* and *C.*

"Push these down and you can mix the hot and cold to your liking, Joe," she said. "I should have it nice and hot."

Joe nodded. He was too overcome with the place to answer for the moment. He'd never seen a contraption like the cloakroom before. All the shining equipment, the glossy tiles, the clean, antiseptic look reminded him of the maternity ward at the hospital.

"Where's the bathtub?" he asked at length.

Mrs. Massiter smiled.

"Not here," she said. "The bathrooms are upstairs."

"Bathrooms?"

"Three." The smile grew bigger. "Would you rather have a bath?"

"No, thanks," said Joe. Three bathrooms! Imagine having *three* baths *and* a shower! When he thought of the painted bathtub behind the curtain in the kitchen at Palfrey Buildings. . . . And what about Mr. Penny? He didn't even have a bath at all. He washed himself down in a wash tub or went to the public baths on Seely Street. Yet this man—a man with three bathrooms, a great house and garden, and everything else—was still not satisfied. He still wanted more.

"Well now, take those wet things off and I'll get them dried." Mrs. Massiter's voice roused him from his thoughts. "By the time you've finished they'll be ready to put on again." She opened the door, and went outside.

"Just leave your clothes by the door, and the maid will bring them back when they're ready. When you're dressed, come to the lounge, and we'll talk over tea."

Twenty minutes later Joe stepped out into the corridor. He felt very clean, even behind the ears, and although he'd liked using the perfumed soap he wished the smell wouldn't linger. Only girls should smell nice. If Mr. Penny could get a whiff of him now he'd call him a sissy. Still, the shower was fun. He'd really enjoyed washing that way, and by the time he'd dried off, his clothes were awaiting him, neatly folded outside the door. He dressed quickly and combed his hair, and it wasn't until he was in the corridor with an appetite for tea that he realized he didn't know where the lounge was.

Mrs. Massiter had led him into the house through a side door and along the thickly carpeted corridor to the cloak-room. So he continued in the same direction. After making one turn, the corridor opened into a square hall. There were doors on either side and another corridor almost opposite sealed off with double doors. Faint culinary sounds issued from these and Joe guessed that the kitchen was behind them. Across the hall a narrow, wrought-iron staircase spiralled to the floor above, but there was no sign of a front door. Below the staircase was a wide door with an oval window. When he looked through he could see the main hall at the end of a broad corridor. He went through, his shoes making no sound on the deep pile carpet that spread to the oak-paneled walls on either side.

The front hall was huge, semi-circular. And Joe had never seen a staircase like this one. It was even grander

55 ❧

than the one in Greenham's town hall. It was all white and so wide you could have driven Smokey and the cart up it and still had room to pass on a bike. It swept down in a shallow fall from a gallery decorated with pictures. Over the center hung a crystal chandelier that seemed to reflect all the colors of the rainbow in the sunlight filtering through the windows at either side of the front door. Around the walls at intervals were small side tables and on some of these stood vases of flowers; others were dressed with small silver ornaments. There were several doors, and on each side of these were tall white alabaster urns with blooms of lilac, rhododendron, and laburnum.

Joe moved out from the corridor and placed himself behind a spray of lilac. He stood there watching and wondering. . . . Which door opened into the lounge?

As he pondered the problem Parker appeared on the landing and came stiffly down the stairs. Joe cringed back behind the spreading blossoms and watched the butler cross the hall and enter a door opposite. Before the door was closed Joe heard Mr. Massiter's voice in the room, and then the great hall was silent and empty again.

It was no use, he decided. No use staying to tea. It wouldn't do any good. He'd told his story to Mrs. Massiter and she might have told her husband, but what difference would it make? What he'd seen of the house and its owner was enough to convince him how hopeless it was to pursue Mr. Penny's cause further. The best thing he could do was to pick up Tinker and go.

With one more furtive look around the hall, he slipped from his hiding place and tiptoed into the corridor, moving swiftly, silently back the way he had come. No one saw him leave the house, and when he reached the potting shed he was relieved to find that Hoskins wasn't there. Tinker was asleep, his coat now as dry as a ship's biscuit. He seemed so exhausted after his escapade that he hardly awoke when Joe spoke to him and put him in his traveling box.

Joe left the shed and moved quietly along a path screened by a yew hedge, past the garage, and then through the shrubs to the drive. There he stopped, peering through a rhododendron bush at the black Rolls-Royce parked in front of the porch. The chauffeur stood at attention, holding open the rear door, the same chauffeur who had driven away from Sparrow Street on Saturday morning. Mr. Massiter came down the steps clutching a briefcase, followed by Parker carrying a small bag. Mr. Massiter stepped into the car, the chauffeur closed the door and took the bag from Parker. Then he slipped behind the wheel and the car glided past Joe's hiding place and out of the drive.

Joe waited till Parker had closed the door, then he moved on across the grass to the drive. He'd nearly reached the gate when a voice from behind brought him up short.

"Joe!"

He turned and there was Mrs. Massiter hurrying toward him from the side of the house.

· *Chapter Seven* ·

She came nearer.

"I've been looking for you, Joe." She glanced down at Tinker's box. "Where are you going?"

"Home," Joe said.

"But I thought you'd agreed to have tea with me."

He stared awkwardly at the ground.

"I don't feel like tea."

"What's the matter, Joe?"

"Nothing."

"Then why are you running away?"

"Not running," he said. "Just going."

"Without even saying good-by?"

He felt miserable. It wasn't her fault the way things had turned out. He didn't know what to say.

Her deep brown eyes were searching his face.

"You mean you were just going to leave without even a word?"

Still he couldn't answer.

"I thought we were friends."

"That's—what—I'd like," he stammered at last.

"Well, what happened? You had the shower—and your clothes were dry?"

"I liked the shower."

"I was expecting you in to tea. I waited and when you didn't come I went to the cloakroom and then to the potting shed. No one had seen you. And here I find you leaving without a word. I don't think you're that kind of a boy. What happened?"

"Nothing—" Joe hesitated. "Nothing happened. I just thought—well, I'd told my story, and I didn't think it would do much good, anyway. So what was the use of staying? Besides, it's getting late, and it's a long way home by bus."

"Well, we'll have tea, and then I'll take you home in the car."

"You'll come back with me—to Sparrow Street?"

"Why not?"

"But . . ." He was so surprised.

"Don't you want me to meet Mr. Penny?"

"Yes," said Joe. "I do."

Lawton drove them back in the Mercédès. It was a sumptuous car. Sinking into the luxury of the back seat beside Mrs. Massiter, with Tinker riding comfortably in his box on the deep pile carpet at his feet, Joe almost forgot that his mission had failed. Or perhaps because he was riding back in the Mercédès with Mrs. Massiter he was semi-conscious of a hope that maybe the mission wasn't finished yet. It could have been that. The tea might have had something to do with it as well. He'd never eaten so much. He was full of cream buns and chocolate cake and hot buttered scones and strawberry jam. And when you're full of those things you take a different view of life. Whatever it was he felt better on the way back than on the way there. Despite Mr. Massiter.

They hadn't talked about him at all. Mostly they talked about Mr. Penny. Joe mentioned the livestock man in Pease Row market because they'd gotten Tinker from him. The livestock man had found the creature, young and helpless, on a business trip to the country, and had brought him back to the market. But there wasn't much call for weasels in London so Mr. Penny had struck a bargain and bought him cheap for Joe. That's how they got around to the country in general and Mrs. Massiter said that she had a small house with a meadow and a stream at the end fringed with willow trees. It was a warm, mellow, brick house overlooking the valley. Joe wanted to know all about it and the countryside, but before Mrs. Massiter could answer Lawton had brought them quietly into Sparrow Street.

Joe told him where to stop, and he pulled up just past

the gates in the fence below the line of billboards.

Joe got out and opened one of the gates, then came back to the car.

"Doesn't look as if Mr. Penny's home yet," he said. "But I'll show you around while we're waiting."

Lawton stood holding open the door as Mrs. Massiter got out. He was looking up at the picture of the pretty girl with not much on advertising the coming attractions at the Hippodrome, and wondering vaguely where the Hippodrome was.

"You can come, too, if you like," Joe told him.

But Lawton didn't like the look of the neighborhood, and he had to think about the car. He wouldn't care to have to explain to the master if it was damaged by hooligans.

"I think I'd better wait out here, thanks all the same," he said.

Mrs. Massiter was very impressed when she got into the yard. She thought she would see piles of junk all over the place, but it was difficult to see it at all, tucked away in the compound covered by a tarpaulin. The timbered outbuildings were neat and tidy, the cobbled yard surprisingly clean, and at the end was the little house with a touch of old England about it. True, the house was chipped a little at the edges, but the red and white paint seemed sparkling fresh, and amid the gray, dilapidated surrounding buildings, it stood out like a treasure. Even as she looked at it she wondered if it might merit preservation as an example of early architecture.

Joe pointed out the cart shed with its leather and brasses, then Smokey's stable, and then he was leading her through the gate between the woodshed and the house.

The difference a few steps could make was quite un-believable. It was like stepping into a different world. By contrast with the plain, austere yard, the vista just through the gate was of a sudden splendor that was almost magical. Everywhere the grass was lush and green. Mellow brick pathways formed winding threads of russet between young and slender trees and a variety of shrubs. There were plantings of broom, lilac, laburnum, and Cupressus, and neat hedges of evergreen. In the air was the faint scent of honeysuckle.

Certainly, from the gate you could see the higher alti-tudes of Carter's old warehouse on the other side, and at the far end, the blank walls of the trolley depot. But once you stepped deeper into the garden these dreary objects were screened by the trees and you might have been out of town right in the heart of the country. Looking back, even the dark walls of the sheds were partially concealed by the meandering stems of rambler roses, except where the low window formed a square of light in Smokey's stable. The main window at the back of the house was the large one on the ground floor and this was framed by two tall lilac shrubs.

Mrs. Massiter was quite overwhelmed by what she saw, and she hadn't seen the animals yet. It was hard to believe that Mr. Penny had achieved such lavish results with what at one time had been a piece of waste ground. As she followed Joe she understood the anguish with which they viewed the end of it all.

"This is the food store." Joe opened the door of a lean-to shed by the garden well. "I set this up," he went on proudly, inviting her to enter. "Mr. Penny takes care of the garden, I look after the animals."

"So they're your pets? You brought them in?"

"Most of them." Joe nodded, following her into the shed.

Inside, the hut was dry and well-ventilated with a rough boarded floor raised off the ground. It was lined with broad shelves and there were hooks from which hung pieces of heavy rope and lengths of string. On one shelf was an old meat safe, others contained a small shovel, a pair of large wooden spoons, three mixing bowls, some metal dishes, and a bucket. Alongside the walls were thick brown paper bags of meal and bran and small sacks of meadow hay and wheat straw, and in the corner was a tub full of chaff. It was all very clean and so tidy it would have done credit to the strictest matron. When Mrs. Massiter remarked on this and the well-stocked larder, Joe told her that animals were most particular about their food. If you wanted to keep them in the pink of condition you had to be careful to feed them the right amount of the right food at regular times. His animals would soon turn up their noses if their food was stale or if mice had been nesting in it. But they were lucky really because a friend of Mr. Penny's was the corn dealer in Casey Street and they got everything from him fresh and cheap.

"You don't get any unwelcome visitors after the food from all these old buildings around you?" asked Mrs. Massiter.

"You mean rats and mice and things like that?"

She nodded, and he pointed through the window in the side of the hut to a large black cat asleep against the wall.

"Not with fellas like him about," he said. "There's another one the same—only ginger. They're strays really. That one's Caution, the other we call Amber. We've never had any trouble since they've been here. O' course, they're a bit on the wild side and they come and go as they please, but mostly they stay."

"Do they get on well with the other animals?"

"They don't show much interest," Joe said, opening the safe. "I s'pose they put up with them. But they can't put up with each other. You never see them together. Caution stays out here and Amber has the run of the yard and the sheds." He smiled. "But that suits us. They keep the pests away from both places."

Mrs. Massiter smiled, too. The more she saw and heard, the more fascinated she became and the more sympathy she felt for the problem they faced.

"Is it feeding time?" she asked.

"Not yet." Joe took a handful of meat scraps from the safe. "I'm just giving Tinker a bit. To settle him after his travels. Will you carry him?"

She took the traveling box, and Joe put the meat in a clean dish and picked up an aluminum jug. Outside, near the wall, was a standpipe. He filled the jug while she waited on the path. Tinker was making scratching noises in his box.

"Come on," Joe said. "I'll show you where he lives."

It was an elaborate cage for a weasel. More like a netted-in compound really. Nicely placed between two dwarf pine trees with shrubs standing back on either side, it was sheltered from the weather. The sides and top were made of strong wire netting and at one end was a folding screen made of canvas that could be adjusted to cover half the run when it rained. Tinker had plenty of furniture to amuse him. There were two small boxes raised off the ground which gave him a choice of snug nests. He could just squeeze through the entrance holes. Placed at various parts of the run were bits of pipe, small branches, stones of all sizes, shelves, and a chestnut log.

Joe leaned over and raised the large door in the run. He placed Tinker's box inside and opened it. Tinker sprang out and ran up on one of the shelves. He watched Joe put down the dish of meat, wash out the drinking bowl, and fill it with fresh water. When the door was lowered, Tinker came down and began to feed and drink. Afterward he sprawled on his back against the log and groomed the sparkling white fur of his belly.

They left him then, and Joe led his guest along a line of evergreens and over a patch of long grass. He was looking about him and treading carefully.

"Mind where you walk," he said. "The tortoise and the hedgehog may be somewhere around here."

But they didn't run across them and the next residents to whom Mrs. Massiter was introduced were the rabbits and guinea pigs. There were a pair of each in two large, straw-lined hutches which were mounted off the ground on wooden supports. Before either of the breeds could be closely inspected, Mrs. Massiter was hit lightly on the shoulder by an acorn. She turned and Joe pointed to a young copper beech tree nearby.

"It's Nutmeg," he explained. "He's got no manners at all. He's always throwing things. Specially acorns. We don't give him many but he seems to hoard them up in

65 ❧

some secret place I can never find."

At first she couldn't see anything through the growth of the tree, then, going nearer, she saw the gray squirrel sitting on his haunches just where a slim bough joined the trunk.

"Nutmeg has the run o' the place the same as the tortoise and the hedgehog," Joe said. "The others only come out at certain times, specially Tinker. Since we got him we have to be a bit careful."

"You mean weasels attack rabbits and guinea pigs and squirrels?" Mrs. Massiter queried.

Joe nodded. "And even swim for fish, too. Just like Tinker did in your pond. But I think in time we'll tame him. That's what we want to do. So they'll all live together like a family."

He stepped up to the tree and called to the squirrel. After some hesitation Nutmeg began to descend slowly. Eventually, he was lying back in Joe's arms while Mrs. Massiter stroked his head and bushed out the tip of his tail.

"He *is* tame," she said. "You can get quite close to them in the park and they come into the garden sometimes, but I've never been able to get near enough to touch one."

"Yes, he's very good," Joe agreed. "But it's a pity about his manners."

He put Nutmeg back in the tree and then stood listening.

"Thought so," he said at length. "Mr. Penny's back."

Mrs. Massiter glanced in the direction of the gate.

"How do you know?"

"Heard Smokey's shoes on the yard. We'd better go out and you can meet them both."

For Mrs. Massiter, meeting Mr. Penny was a new experience. A warm, pleased-to-meet-you experience. He was picturesque in appearance, a little old-fashioned, but there was nothing artificial about him. He was a small man but obviously strong of character, and although he must have had his full share of living and bargaining in a competitive world, he had a simple dignity and something of the innocence of Joe.

Joe could see she was impressed when he introduced them.

So was Mr. Penny. He took off his Panama hat and inclined his head and shoulders slightly in the form of a bow, and didn't know whether to offer his hand, especially as it was a bit on the grubby side from loading the cart. But in the end he did, pointing out that it was hardly clean enough to shake a lady's hand. Mrs. Massiter brushed aside his excuses and they shook hands warmly, and it was not until then that Mr. Penny fully understood the significance of the name.

"Mrs. Massiter?" he repeated, looking from one to the other a little anxiously, and decidedly puzzled. "I saw the big car outside . . ."

"You've already met *Mister* Massiter," Joe said.

"You mean—this is the lady of the gentleman who came on Saturday morning . . . ?" Mr. Penny, although unruffled, was very much out of his depth.

"That's right," Mrs. Massiter said gently. "Joe came up to see us this afternoon."

"*You* went up to see them, Joe?" Mr. Penny was looking most concerned.

"I wanted to explain—about all this—and us." Joe's

voice trembled a bit, but he didn't think Mr. Penny would be angry in front of Mrs. Massiter. "I took Tinker."

"We had a long talk," she said. "And found we had a great deal in common."

"And I had a shower," Joe said, when he saw how well Mr. Penny was taking it.

"I wanted to meet you and see the garden and the animals," she went on. "So Joe and I and Tinker came back together."

"Well, I never!" Mr. Penny was still rather flabbergasted.

"You and Joe must be very proud of your achievement here," Mrs. Massiter continued. "The garden is beautiful."

"Well, thank you, ma'am." He was twisting the brim of his Panama hat quite unconsciously. "I'm happy it gives you pleasure. But I hope you'll forgive our manners—keeping you out in the yard. Will you come into the house for a cup o' tea?"

"We've had tea," Joe said. "You should have seen what there was!"

"Thank you for the invitation, Mr. Penny," she said. "But I ought to be going." She looked over his shoulder at the donkey and the laden cart. "And you've work to do, I can see."

"You must speak to Smokey before you go," Joe said.

They moved down the yard and she spoke to Smokey who stood very still between the shafts. He liked all the fuss but he would rather have had a meal so he wasn't sorry when the procession moved on.

They went with her to the gates and Mr. Penny invited her to come again and perhaps next time she would stay to tea. She said she would look forward to that, and to a more leisurely look at their garden.

Mr. Penny stood at the gate ready to wave good-by. Joe went with her to the car. Lawton got out and opened the door. Joe offered his hand and she clasped it firmly in her own.

"You'll come again, won't you?" he said.

"That is a promise, Joe."

"When?"

"Soon."

"Could soon be Saturday?"

"If that would suit you and Mr. Penny."

"That's the best day of the lot."

"It's settled then."

"And . . ." He wasn't sure how to say it with Lawton standing there.

She leaned toward him. "What is it, Joe?"

"Well—now that you've seen the place—and everything—would you—could you try and help and—well, you know what I mean—"

"I know," she said. "That is a promise, too."

· *Chapter Eight* ·

The contractors moved into Carter's warehouse toward the end of June. You could hear them banging and drilling, and brick and concrete crumbling when you stood in Mr. Penny's yard. The noise even seeped into the house.

In a matter of days the dust was rising and a gray film settling on the lush greenery in the garden. The roses were out but they were losing their bloom. White ones became off-white and the reds paled to a grayish pink. Even the animals noticed the change in the air. They were restless. Sniffing. It was as if they had caught the scent of some calamity.

Only the cats were at ease. Caution and Amber were accustomed to insecurity. They'd grown up in the alleys and the factory yards, driven from pillar to post, until they had found the sanctuary in Sparrow Street. They were indifferent to change, and accepted placidly what the changes brought.

Mrs. Massiter had come on Saturday and had stayed to tea, but she hadn't brought any news. She'd taken some photographs of the garden and of Joe and Mr. Penny which she said she'd place before her husband at the first opportunity. She was hoping the pictures might help her to help matters. But that was some time before the contractors moved in, and Mr. Penny had heard nothing from her since. He had heard from the company's lawyers again. And Mr. Hawkins, the borough surveyor, had paid a call to let Mr. Penny know that the development committee would soon make an inspection of the site. He strongly advised acceptance of a private offer.

Joe didn't know much about all this at the time. He was trying to cope with his own troubles, which were quite apart from the main trouble on Sparrow Street. Aunt Ethel and the new boy were not doing too well. She'd come out of the hospital and then gone back in again, taking the baby with her. Liz was better, and had begun looking for a job. The school inspector had been around to check on Joe's absence, and he had to go back to his class. On top of all that, Uncle Bert had broken his leg and was in a hospital in Australia. So altogether it was a pretty fine state of affairs.

In spite of it all Joe still managed to get over to Sparrow Street each day, but the visits were brief and there was little time for leisurely cups of tea in Mr. Penny's kitchen. Most times Mr. Penny wasn't even there when Joe called. Joe went in the morning before going to school and Mr. Penny had already left on his rounds. Joe fed the animals then and also at lunchtime and after school.

On the evenings when he didn't go to see Aunt Ethel, he spent more time at Sparrow Street, and he and Mr. Penny would tend the garden and the animals together until twilight. Then they would sit in the kitchen with a cup of tea and buttered toast or some Gorgonzola cheese and water biscuits. Sometimes Mr. Penny would pour himself a Guinness or a Nut Brown ale, but usually he made do with tea.

That was the time when Mr. Penny would glance at the morning paper. In the evening. There was little opportunity to read anything before that except letters and bills. So he would spread the paper out on the kitchen table and lodge his gold-rimmed glasses on the bridge of his nose and read out some news item or comment which caught his interest.

One such evening when Joe was munching a biscuit and staring out of the window at the darkening sky, Mr. Penny turned a page and then spilled the tea from his cup as he clashed it against the saucer in agitation.

"Bless me soul!" he exclaimed. "Look who's in the paper!"

Joe couldn't understand all the excitement. It was unlike

Mr. Penny to get ruffled at all, let alone by anything in the paper.

"Who is it?" Joe looked across at him.

"Come here, my lad, and see."

Joe went over.

It was the gossip page and there were three pictures, one at the top and two lower down. The one at the top was a head and shoulders portrait of a woman and the face looked familiar but he couldn't place it.

"See who it is?" Mr. Penny was pointing at the top picture.

"Who?" Joe still couldn't see.

"Why, Mrs. Massiter, o' course!"

"Well!" Joe took a hard look. "So it is!" It was either a bad picture or an old one; it certainly wasn't very clear, but he should have recognized her large shadowy eyes.

"Couldn't believe it myself till I read the name underneath," Mr. Penny admitted, and went on silently reading the long caption.

"What's she in the paper for?" Joe asked. "What's it say?"

"Ah!" Mr. Penny said without looking up, continuing to read to himself. Then in a low voice, "Bless me soul! Fancy!" And again, a moment later, to himself and rather sadly, " 'Tis a pity such things have to happen."

"What things?" Joe was impatient now. "What's it about?"

Mr. Penny looked up at last.

"They're parting, Joe."

"Who?"

"Mrs. Massiter and her husband."

"They are? What for?"

"Doesn't rightly say."

"What *does* it say then?"

"Listen and I'll read it." Mr. Penny adjusted the delicate balance of his glasses and slowly began to read aloud, " 'Property tycoon Arnold Massiter, who is chairman of Winthrop Property Developments, Limited, and a director of three other London companies, has separated from his wife, Laura, thirty-six—above . . .' "

"*Thirty-six above*—what's that mean?" Joe leaned closer.

"Well, *thirty-six*, that's how old she is—and *above*—that's in brackets and refers to the picture. Shall I go on or will you read it yourself?"

"You read it. You're better."

"Well then, where was I? Ah, yes. . . . 'And she will be moving out of their London home on Eleigh Place. Before her marriage Mrs. Massiter was Laura Wheaton, only child of the late Mr. and Mrs. Wheaton, who controlled a small hotel group. After their tragic death in an air crash six years ago, the company went into liquidation.

" 'At forty-seven, Mr. Massiter is recognized as one of the youngest and most successful tycoons in the real estate world, and his company is responsible for much of the new building in London. The couple were married nearly ten years ago, and there was one child, who died in infancy.' " Mr. Penny looked up and sighed. He took off his glasses and wiped his eyes with the back of his hand. "Well," he murmured sadly. "It just shows you. Such a nice woman."

"No wonder we haven't heard from her," Joe said, looking wistfully out the window.

"It just shows you what happens to people who don't put people first." Mr. Penny was looking absently at the caption without his glasses. "The most successful tycoon . . ." he muttered.

"Mrs. Massiter's so different from—from him. D'you think she's changed much? I mean, she seems nice and friendly. D'you think she's always been like that?"

"I reckon she has. It's her nature."

"Then why did she marry someone with a nature like Mr. Massiter's?"

"There's no explaining what women will do sometimes, Joe. Especially when it comes to men. But I think myself that when they got married, Mr. Massiter wasn't like he is today."

"You mean he hadn't got the money and the power?"

"Not as much as he has now."

"And you think it's gone to his head? Made him greedy?"

"It could have changed him, Joe. If you intend going to the top you've no time for anything else. And when you rise that far you're so busy staying there you can't even stop to relax. You have to keep going just to stand still."

Mr. Penny was good at understanding. Especially people, and the things they did. He seldom said a cross word about others and nearly always made excuses for those who were to blame. There was so much unhappiness in the world that even his own happiness was tinged with sadness that he could do so little about it. Joe thought his own action in going to see Mr. Massiter without saying a word had upset Mr. Penny at first, but if it had, he didn't show it. Not a rebuke even. Meeting Mr. Massiter might have had something to do with that.

"It's a pity, Joe," Mr. Penny was saying. "But I reckon we've got to make up our minds that we shan't see her any more."

"Why not? Why should that make any difference?"

"Well, she's got to get out of her home. She'll have so many problems of her own you can't expect her to think about ours as well."

"I can't believe that. She's our friend." Joe frowned, and then his face puckered into a smile. "Besides," he added, "she promised."

Later that week, Saturday in fact, Joe went around to Sparrow Street as usual, but with better news from the home front. While Mr. Penny was making the mid-morning pot of tea, Joe told him that Aunt Ethel and the new boy were coming home on Sunday. They were better but the doctor wanted them to go away somewhere to convalesce. So they were going to stay with Aunt Maisie in Brighton.

"Aunt Maisie?" queried Mr. Penny, slipping the blue cosy on the teapot. "Your Aunt Ethel's sister? I thought she lived in the Midlands."

"So she did. But Uncle Fred's been transferred, and they've just moved to Brighton. She came up to the hospital yesterday."

"Well—that's really something, Joe. The sea air will

do Aunt Ethel and the baby no end of good." He began to pour the tea. "What about Liz?"

"She's going, too. Aunt Maisie reckons she'll get a job easy in Brighton now that the summer season's starting."

"She could do with a change after them measles," Mr. Penny nodded.

"So Aunt Ethel said . . ." Joe hesitated.

Mr. Penny put the pot on the stove. He came back to the table and invited Joe to take one of the cups. Joe took one, and Mr. Penny sat down.

"What did Aunt Ethel say?" he prompted.

Joe fingered his spoon.

"Well, she said, seeing as the place is empty, or will be next week, you could have the use of it if things got so—well, you know—if anything happened sudden-like. . . ."

"That's very kind of her." Mr. Penny was touched. "To think o' me when she's been through so much herself."

"And it's nice and handy," Joe pointed out.

"It is that," he nodded. "What are you going to do? You going to Brighton?"

"Oh, no! You know I wouldn't leave you—and the animals. Besides, there's school," he added with a grin. "I shall be all right. I can look after myself. I'll be around here all my spare time and just sleep at Palfrey Buildings."

"Lor' bless you, that would be a silly thing to do when there's room enough for you here." He stirred his tea slowly, and there was that soft twinkle in his eye. "So thank Aunt Ethel very much and tell her you'll stay wi' me."

In the afternoon when the hammering and the drilling

77 ✂

in Carter's warehouse had finally stopped for the day, they went into the garden and syringed the dust off some of the roses and evergreens.

The dust that settled over everything as the innards of the warehouse came down and the tubular scaffolding went up always made Mr. Penny upset. It seemed to Joe that it made him more determined than ever to remain on Sparrow Street and defend his rights, although he knew it was like fighting a rearguard action for a piece of territory the troops had given up trying to hold long ago.

Joe often went across the garden to see how close the contractors had come to the other side of the warehouse wall. For the wall was still standing, like a last battlement about to fall. There were small holes in the brickwork in places, and at one end, where the corner of the building faced Fowler's Alley, there was an old door which had been torn from its hinges before the contractors moved in. The wall formed the boundary of the garden except for a few yards on the alley side, but it was easy to get over the wire fence that Mr. Penny had erected there if you wanted to reach the doorway in the wall.

Sometimes Joe looked through when all the men were working there. Other times he looked in the evening or on Saturday afternoon when the site and all the equipment lay waiting in silence. And whenever he looked, it was always for some way in which he might stop the tide of progress flooding over the garden. But the more he looked the more he realized there was no way.

On Saturday afternoon, Joe wandered over after leaving Mr. Penny with two fresh pails of water for the syringe, and returned in time to fill them again.

"What's it look like over there?" Mr. Penny inquired, giving the floribundas a gentle squirt. He had never been to see for himself.

"They've got a bit of the building up right on the farther side," Joe said. "There's still a lot of holes at this end, and lots of steel pipes. There's scaffolding all over the place, and some iron girders and things on a great slab of concrete. Looks as if they're going to make a big crane."

Mr. Penny tipped back his Panama hat and wiped his hot forehead with a handkerchief.

"Seems a lot o' use doing this, don't it, Joe?" he murmured.

Joe couldn't think of anything to say to that.

Mr. Penny put his hat straight.

"Time to wash this dust out of our mouths, my lad," he said, slipping the syringe under his arm and picking up the empty pails. "Let's go in to tea."

It was while Mr. Penny was struggling to open the obstinate top of a pot of fish paste that the knock came on the kitchen door. Joe was cutting bread.

"Oh, dear," Mr. Penny sighed. "I expect that's Tom Mason. He said he might call this afternoon with some new shoes for Smokey. Open the door, Joe."

Joe opened the door. And they couldn't believe their eyes.

Mrs. Massiter stood there.

· Chapter Nine ·

Mrs. Massiter wouldn't have any fish paste. She wouldn't eat anything at all. Just a cup of tea would be very nice.

Joe and Mr. Penny couldn't eat anything, either. Their pleasure was so great at seeing her again it had taken away any appetite they had. They wanted to know how she was and where she had been and what had happened, but they didn't like to ask her. They waited politely for her to tell them.

She told them she had left the house in London and

had moved to the country. That was why they hadn't heard from her. There had been so many things to do, and this was the first opportunity she had had of getting in touch again.

"I don't know whether you've heard, but I've left my husband." She spoke without any sign of emotion. "It was the only thing to do. He made it impossible for us to go on."

"We saw it in the paper." Mr. Penny nodded sympathetically.

"There was a picture of you," Joe said quietly.

Mr. Penny cleared his throat. You could see he was a bit embarrassed, but he had to voice what was worrying him.

"I hope, ma'am, this unfortunate affair is not due to your interest in us."

"It would have ended like this, Mr. Penny, whatever interest I had. We were—incompatible, I think that is the word they use." A faint smile touched the corners of her mouth. "But I haven't come to seek sympathy for myself or to talk about my domestic affairs. I wanted to give you my address in the country and to suggest you make use of my lawyer."

"Is that the house in the country you were telling me about?" Joe asked.

"Yes. It is my own little possession."

"Use of your lawyer?" Mr. Penny could see that she didn't want to talk about the separation, and she was too generous a person to tell the plain truth about her husband. But it was obvious she was entirely on their side.

She nodded. "I think he will be able to help you, cer-

81 ✎

tainly advise you. Have you got the deeds to this property?"

"Well, yes, they're here. Hmm . . . somewhere about." Mr. Penny stroked his chin. "Ah, o' course, in the old tin chest they'll be. Haven't opened that for years."

"The house and garden have been in your family for a long time?"

"Before my gran'father's day. And in my father's time —and before, I think—the garden was rented out."

"Now that's the kind of thing I'm getting at. It's possible there is a clause in the old deeds, an ancient right concerning this plot which might convey it for all time as open ground."

"I hadn't thought o' that," Mr. Penny admitted.

"Open ground?" Joe didn't understand.

"No building permitted," Mrs. Massiter explained. "I'm not saying it's likely, but there is always a faint hope. Clauses of that kind may be overlooked or erased, concealed or just forgotten."

"I haven't looked at the deeds in years," Mr. Penny said thoughtfully. "But I don't recall anything o' that sort."

"You may not have all the documents. When it comes to property and legal affairs there are all kinds of important angles that the layman doesn't see or understand. In this case, it's well worth investigating, and Mr. Boddy's an expert on such matters."

"Mr. *Boddy?*" The name seemed to amuse Joe.

"The lawyer. He's a very good friend of mine. The senior partner of Boddy, Bagworth, and Stringer in Chancery Lane." She smiled at Joe. "You'll be meeting him when he calls."

"We're very grateful, I'm sure, ma'am, for all your help," Mr. Penny said. "And I'll take any advice your wise friend likes to give me."

"We mustn't lose any time. He'll probably want to take away the deeds, and will need to know the lawyer who has acted for you and your family in the past."

"Oh, dear!" Mr. Penny exclaimed sadly. "I'm afraid he's dead and I haven't had one since."

"Never mind. So long as you can give Mr. Boddy his name, he will trace any documents and other relevant information." Mrs. Massiter opened her handbag and took out a small diary. "I'd better arrange his visit for Monday—would that suit you, Mr. Penny?"

"That would suit me, ma'am," he said. "There's some sorting out to be done in the compound. I can be here all day."

"Splendid." She began to write in her diary. "I'll suggest the morning—say, eleven-thirty, or if he's engaged then, any time after that?"

"Any time," Mr. Penny said.

Mrs. Massiter put the diary back in her handbag and came up with a visiting card. She wrote an address and telephone number on the back.

"Whenever you want to get in touch with me, this is my new home." She showed Mr. Penny the card. "Although just for a time while I need to be in town I've taken a room at the Onslow Court Hotel in Russell Square. That's the hotel phone number." She jotted the figures down on the face of the card and handed it to him.

Mr. Penny thanked her and took the card.

"Whereabouts in the country is it?" Joe asked. "Too

83 ✄

far for Smokey to walk?"

"Well, yes." She smiled. "It's a long walk, but no great distance by car or train."

"Elmbridge . . . Suffolk." Mr. Penny was looking at the card and rolling the words on his tongue as if they tasted nice. "Refined country, I reckon."

"You'll remember my telling you, Joe, the house overlooked a valley," Mrs. Massiter went on. "The name on my gate is *Valley End*. I hope you and Mr. Penny will come and see me there."

"Yes, I remember," Joe nodded.

"We'd like to come and see you there," Mr. Penny said.

Mrs. Massiter went out the way she came in—through the yard. They walked with her to the car. It was a different model and there was no sign of Lawton. She was driving it herself. Mr. Penny opened the driver's door for her.

"Remember," she said when she was behind the wheel, "Give Mr. Boddy all the help you can and all the letters and inquiries you've had offering to buy the property. I shall be keeping in touch with Mr. Boddy, and I'll be calling here again, but don't hesitate to contact me if you have any news."

Mr. Penny took off his Panama hat and shook her hand. He couldn't seem to find words to express his gratitude.

"I don't know how to thank you. . . ." he began.

"Don't thank me—I should be thanking you." She looked up at him through the open window, her dark eyes large and solemn. "All my life I've wanted to do something worthwhile, Mr. Penny. I've never had the courage to break out and seek the opportunity. I think I've finally found the opportunity now."

They stood on the curb and watched her drive away down Sparrow Street. Not until the car had disappeared behind the wall of the old trolley depot did Mr. Penny put on his hat again.

"Such a good woman, Joe," he said. "And no one to appreciate her but us."

On Monday at noon when Joe left school for the lunch break, he ran straight over to Sparrow Street to see if the lawyer had come. He saw the car outside the front door and hurried in the back way. There was no one in the kitchen, so he made for the parlor and met Mr. Boddy in the hall.

Mr. Penny introduced them. "This is the young friend I was telling you about," he added.

"G'morning, sir," said Joe.

"Good morning." Mr. Boddy nodded briskly. He was a rather fierce and official-looking man in a dark suit. He carried a black briefcase and had very sharp eyes that Joe reckoned could see through any document.

"Well, I think that concludes our business for the moment, Mr. Penny." He edged toward the front door. "Remember my advice—don't make any comment or take any action until you've consulted me. Any further letters or inquiries concerning the property must all be referred to me."

"You can be sure I'll do that, sir." Mr. Penny opened the door. "Good day, and thank you."

When they were on their own in the kitchen Joe wanted to know how the interview had gone.

"He's a clever one, that Mr. Boddy," Mr. Penny told him. "If there's anything to be found in our favor, I'm sure he'll find it. I told him all I could and gave him everything to do wi' the place. All we can do now is wait and see." He wiped the oilcloth-covered table with a duster and then took a linen tablecloth from a drawer. "Are you staying for a bit o' dinner wi' me, Joe?"

"Can't do that, Mr. Penny, thanks. Aunt Ethel's expecting me home."

"How is she today?"

"Fine. She's going to Brighton on Wednesday."

"Wednesday, eh?" Mr. Penny smiled. "O' course, no sense in hanging about London when she's a chance of sea air. You going to see them all off?"

"I s'pose so."

"Good," Mr. Penny said. "Then you can bring your things over after they've gone."

Joe took his things over in two paper bags. They were the only containers left when Aunt Ethel and Liz had finished packing. They took a taxi to the station and as soon as they'd driven away, Joe picked up his bags and hurried to Sparrow Street. The clock in the hall was striking five when he let himself into the kitchen, and he ran upstairs to unpack, for Mr. Penny had not yet returned from his rounds and Joe wanted to surprise him with the table set for tea.

His room was a small one at the back. It had a narrow white iron bedstead and a pink quilt. There was a marble-topped washstand in front of the window with a huge china jug and bowl and a real wardrobe with two doors

and a long mirror in each. He put the bags on the bed and
went to the window to take a look over the garden, and
the first thing he noticed was the crane.

Tall and gaunt it stood, its slender framework running
up into the sky, towering high above the wall of Carter's
warehouse. He hadn't noticed it before. It must have gone
up since Monday; but it was not working yet. The long
jib with its traveling cradle spread high on either side of
the tower remained motionless, for there was no one in
the cabin beneath. But they hadn't knocked off work on
the site; Joe could hear the usual noises through the closed
window. And there was a man up on the wall. Joe didn't
see him at first because he was right at the end and he only
had eyes for the crane. But now the man was plain enough,
and he was using a pick to chip away the brickwork at the
top. Even as he watched the man suddenly appeared to
sway and although he regained his balance, the pick left
his hands and fell into the garden.

Joe ran downstairs and through the garden to the
boundary. He began to walk alongside the warehouse
wall toward Fowler's Alley, searching the grass and
bushes. When he was getting close to the point where the
wire fence started, a man in blue dungarees and a white
steel helmet appeared in the doorway and stepped over
the fence. Joe guessed he was the man who'd dropped
the pick. He was tall and brawny and he moved slowly,
his eyes cast down, so he didn't see Joe until they were
within feet of each other.

"Weel, an' be-divil-to-yer, the place is inhabited!" The
voice was strong and Irish and there was a merry sparkle
in the blue eyes as he looked at Joe. "It's a fine bit o'

country hereabouts I'm thinking." His glance swept over the garden. "And what do I find in it but a leprechaun right before me eyes!"

Joe laughed, although he wasn't sure what a leprechaun was. It was the stranger's manner that amused him.

"If I'm trespassing on sacred ground you must find it in your heart to forgive me, boy, for I'm looking for me pick, d'you see?"

"I saw it fall," Joe said. "I was at my bedroom window in the house, back there."

"D'you mean to say you live in this park then?"

"Well, yes, with my friend, Mr. Penny." Joe giggled.

"And who might he be?"

"He's the junk man, and he owns all this."

"Does he now? So he won't be minding me looking for me pick which wouldn't have the value of a bit o' junk."

"I came out to help you."

"Be-divil-you-did. So it's kindness itself I be lookin' at, to be sure. Weel now, how right I was for as soon as I clapped eyes on ye, I says to mesel' now there's me boy, I says. What's your name?"

"Joe."

"Weel now, Joe, meet Mick." He held out a great dusty hand and Joe put his into it. "Mick Haggity from Dublin."

"I'm glad you didn't fall as well," Joe said warmly. "I thought you were going to lose your balance."

"Mick Haggity lose his balance?" he scoffed. "Not even when he's full o' beer on Saturday night." He leaned closer. "I'll tell ye somethin', Joe. I was only foolin' up there." He glanced toward the top of the wall.

"You were?" Joe couldn't believe it. "But I thought you were gonna fall. You dropped your pick."

"For the foreman's benefit, it was," he said darkly. "D'you see now, Joe, I'm not a demolisher doing a laborer's job. Erector's mate is what I am. Steel. But what happens this afternoon?"

"What happens?"

"Run out of supplies we did. Wi' the drivers on strike, no deliveries, d'you see? So what the divil does the foreman do? He gets the mates on other jobs. Weel now, if that isn't agin the rules, I'm not Mick Haggity. The wall's gotta come down, he says. So he sends me an' some o' the boys up to start chippin'. Weel now, that's agin me rights, Joe. An' I tells the boys, if that's the game then we're gonna strike. D'you see that, Joe? We've gotta stick up for our rights."

"That's what I say," Joe said. "And I wish you'd go on strike."

"You do now?" Mick was very surprised. "What difference can it make to you?"

"Well, the building would stop, wouldn't it?"

"Most o' it, to be sure."

"That would give Mr. Penny and me a chance to stick up for *our* rights."

"*Your* rights?"

"Yes. The man owning the new building you're putting up wants to take this place over as well," Joe said, and quickly he told Mick the whole story. "So you see how it is," he finished. "And we don't know what to do."

Mick Haggity drew a deep breath.

"Weel, now, 'tis a right problem you have to be sure,"

he conceded. "You can't do much against officials and moneybags except go on strike. Which don't apply in your case." His deep brow puckered and he suddenly stepped aside, bent down in a patch of long grass and came up with his pick. He twisted it thoughtfully in his hand. "You and Mr. Penny have the devil of a problem there, Joe. It's public support ye'll be needin'. Public sympathy ye want, but you gotta do somethin' to get in the news afore the public can ever hear your story. If you can get the newspapers and television behind ye, then the rest is easy. Get the public up in arms on your side, then there's no stopping 'em, begorrah."

"How d'you do that?" Joe was very interested.

"Get into the papers first, to be sure, wi' a good image."

"Image?"

"Be a hero. Concoct something sensational."

"Concoct? What's that?"

"Make it up. D'you see now? Do something heroic. Or pretend to."

"Like what?"

"Like stopping a runaway horse."

"Where're you gonna find a runaway horse?"

"Take the first horse you see, me boy, and start it running yourself." He shrugged his huge shoulders. "Or rescue—what about a rescue—"

"*Haggity!*" The voice cut Mick Haggity short. It came from up on the wall. A thin man in white overalls was looking down on them.

"I'm commin'!" the Irishman roared, and then, quieter, "The divil-wi-ye, he'll be askin' for a bloody nose, he will." He scowled up at the man on the wall and Joe guessed he was the foreman.

"We'll be meeting again, Mick?" Joe pleaded.

Haggity moved toward the fence. "To be sure we will, me boy," he said. "And just you remember now, not to lose heart."

After that Joe couldn't think of anything else but what the Irishman had said. About doing something sensational, that is. It was on his mind all evening. But he didn't say anything to Mr. Penny. Mr. Penny would never agree to concocting something sensational or heroic even if it would save his home and garden. Mr. Penny wouldn't dream of concocting anything at all. Joe knew he'd have to keep it to himself, but at the moment he couldn't think of anything sensational to concoct. And when he went to bed he lay awake a long time, peering at the dark cracks in the ceiling which the moonlight splashed with silver, and trying to think of something he could do to get into the papers, for the public's support.

It wasn't easy to say how long he'd been asleep when the cats awakened him. At first he thought he was dreaming, but the violent sounds gradually seeped into his drowsy brain and he suddenly realized they came from outside.

He got up and hurried to the open window, anxious lest some flea-bitten intruder was attacking Caution. But when he looked down into the garden he could see in the moonlight that the attacker was Amber, who had come in from the yard. Caution was the defender although they were not actually fighting. They crouched, eyeing each other as if ready to spring, and bawling insults at the top of their voices.

Joe called to them softly and then began waving his arms. After a while Amber, swearing loudly, backed slowly away toward his own territory beyond the garden gate. Caution sat down and silently watched him go.

It was quiet again. But Joe didn't go back to bed. He stood, staring out of the window at the crane. Its fretwork tower was silhouetted against the sky, and its long, horizontal jib seemed to overshadow the garden, a gigantic steel finger suspended in space.

His gaze dropped to Caution in the garden and as it rose to focus on the crane once more, the interrupted words of the Irishman came back to him . . . *Like stopping a runaway horse. . . . Or rescue—what about a rescue. . . .* Rescue of *what?* An animal? A cat—up a tree? They called the fire brigade for that. It got in the papers. There weren't any trees tall enough for miles around Sparrow Street. But there was the crane. A cat up a crane. . . . Rescued by a boy. That was sensational. . . .

It was the answer to the problem. He had to concoct it. The rescue of one of the cats. From the top of the crane. . . .

· *Chapter Ten* ·

The school term ended the last week in July. That was the week things started to hum. And the weather was so bad you might just as well have been at school, if you were thinking of summer holidays. Nothing but wind and rain, and when the sun did shine it was as if it shone through brown paper. Showers, the forecast said, and gale warnings, and bright intervals; a very unsettled period.

But the weather wasn't half so unsettling as events in Sparrow Street. The empty toy factory opposite Mr.

Penny's yard had had the developers snooping around. The old trolley depot at the end of the street had the demolishers in, and the last of Carter's warehouse wall was toppled as the new building went up. But the most unsettling event of all was Mr. Boddy's failure to find a loophole in the documents concerning Mr. Penny's home and garden.

He'd made a thorough investigation. He'd traced the successors of the late lawyer who'd handled the property in the past, and had delved back through Mr. Penny's ancestors, almost to the ones who'd come from some foreign sunny land. He'd even talked with officials of the borough council. But it was no use. When Mr. Boddy called on Mr. Penny, it was to announce the failure of his mission, and to advise Mr. Penny to accept the offer from Winthrop Property Developments, Limited, but to leave all negotiations to Boddy, Bagworth, and Stringer.

Joe wasn't there when he called, so he heard the news from Mr. Penny. It was a very sad start to the holidays. Just when everyone else was singing their heads off (in spite of the weather) and planning excursions to Southend and Clacton, all Joe could think of was the end of the line.

Joe wished he could have done something sooner about the cat and the crane. He hadn't been determined enough, that was the trouble. It wasn't that he was afraid, it was just that he'd been waiting and hoping for Mr. Boddy to bring about a miracle.

But Joe reckoned now it would be little short of a miracle if he could get one of the cats up the crane. He'd been up himself as far as the control cabin, and he hadn't enjoyed it. He'd made the climb after dark when the site had been deserted, and the wind and the rain had prevented him reaching the jib. He hadn't worried about the dark so much, or even the rain, but the wind had been frightening. It had hurled itself at the tower until the spidery frame had trembled all around him. Gusting through the steel fretwork, it had shrieked at the ladder, threatening to tear him away. He'd climbed down as quickly as he could, depressed by the thought that even if he could get Caution or Amber safely up to the jib in Tinker's traveling box, he could never leave the creature exposed there while the wind blew. No animal could hold on until he made the rescue.

He wanted to talk to Mick Haggity about it, but he hadn't seen the Irishman since their first meeting. He didn't know whether he was on strike or had been fired or was just plain sick. He was nowhere to be seen on the site, anyway, and what with the weather and Mr. Boddy's news which now left so little time, it looked as if Joe's idea would collapse before it started.

Mrs. Massiter came the day after Joe's holidays began. She arrived early, for she had spent the night at the Onslow Court Hotel. Mr. Boddy had called on her there, and had told her the result of his investigations. The failure to find a solution had saddened her. But they had done all they could. Now all that was left was to accept the inevitable, and in this regard she thought she might still be able to help by making them welcome at Valley End.

"I have so much room there," she continued. "A large

garden and a meadow. All the pets would have space to move about and country air to breathe."

Mr. Penny was grateful that she should still have his concern at heart, but at the moment he could not see or think beyond Sparrow Street. No invitation or kindness could make up for losing his home. There was a quiet determination in his blue eyes and a firmness about his voice that you would expect in a man who, now that the end was near, intended to go down fighting.

"I want to see this through," he said. "Either in this house or close by. While I am here there is still a hope. I'm sure you understand, ma'am, why I can't bring myself to leave until the very last."

"Of course. Of course I understand," she said. "I just wanted you to know that my house is there when the time comes." She turned her eyes on Joe. "But what about the animals? If the time is so short, oughtn't we to consider them now? You and I could take them down and get them settled."

"I don't want to leave Mr. Penny," Joe said anxiously.

"Don't you get aworryin' about me, lad," Mr. Penny smiled. "We don't just have ourselves to consider. Mrs. Massiter's right. We've got to make some arrangement about the animals." His smile broadened but you could see it was a little bit sad at the corners. "They're mainly your stock, Joe. You gotta look after their welfare."

"O' course, I'm gonna do that," Joe said.

"You won't have to leave, Joe," Mrs. Massiter pointed out. "At least, only for a night. We could take them down, say tomorrow, and drive back the next day."

"That would be a great relief." Mr. Penny nodded.

"We wouldn't take the cats, not now?" Joe needed them where they were.

"I'm afraid they're too independent to settle anywhere else." Mr. Penny sighed.

"And you'll still need Smokey?" Joe asked.

"I got my rounds to do," Mr. Penny said.

"Well, let's decide on who's going," Mrs. Massiter suggested. "And then you can get them ready for traveling."

"Let's see . . ." Joe gazed out the window. "Tinker . . . I'd better get that old cage ready for him. There's more room in that than his traveling box." Lucky he remembered in time he'd want that on the crane. "The rabbits and guinea pigs can go in their hutches, and I'll fix the top on that little basket and Nutmeg can travel inside. The tortoise and the hedgehog won't be any trouble in cardboard boxes."

"Will you be able to fit them all in?" Mr. Penny asked Mrs. Massiter.

"I think we shall manage," she said.

They managed all right. Set out on the spacious floor in the back of the car there was room to spare, even with the small bags of feed Joe had packed from the food store. Mrs. Massiter drove carefully. She'd never driven animals before and she did not want to make the ride uncomfortable.

Joe sat beside her. His face was as long as the rain-washed street as they drove along the Mile End Road. He kept an eye on the passengers in the back for any sign of restlessness, but he felt pretty sure none of them would be sick. Normally, he'd have been quite excited. Going down to the country. But this was different. It was like

97 ❧

running away from home. He knew it wasn't exactly that this time. He'd be back in a few hours. Yet taking the animals out of the garden was like saying good-by forever.

They stopped in Colchester for tea. But Joe didn't feel like eating. It was a nice place with old oak beams and homemade scones but it didn't make any difference. Mrs. Massiter remarked that he might manage a smile. And he did his best for her sake. But how could you smile when you remembered Mr. Penny's face? The way he'd stood there as they left the yard. He seemed suddenly to have grown older. The gentle lines here and there had become deeper, longer. The soft twinkle in his blue eyes blurred with sadness. How could you smile when you could still see him standing there? A lonely figure in a Panama hat.

For the rest of the way the sun shone fitfully. The rain had stopped, but all around were dark clouds shot now and then with streaks of lightning. The wind whistled lightly over the car and sparrows took wing from the narrow road as they approached. The colors of the countryside were fresh and clear, and the sights and sounds should have brought a new wonder to Joe, but he couldn't really take them in. His mind was brimming over with other things.

Valley End was a mellow brick house with a red-tiled roof and a tall brick chimney. It had crooked gables and sloping floors and many windows, each filled with a lovely view. There were flowers and shrubs and a tidy lawn, bounded at the end by fir and poplar and chestnut.

In the distance across the meadow and beyond the willow-fringed stream was a farm. It was right in the heart of the country, where Joe had always wished to be, but now that he was there all he wanted was to get back to Sparrow Street.

Still, it was nice to meet the housekeeper and the handyman. Mrs. Potter was a motherly soul and took to Joe right away. So did her husband. They lived in the cottage just down the lane and maintained the house and garden for Mrs. Massiter. They hadn't any children, but they had a border-collie who was mothering some pups and that took Joe's mind off things a bit.

Then there was the unloading to do, so he had to concentrate. Mr. Potter arranged everything in what he called the barn, a small, thatched-roofed outbuilding. It was free from drafts, well ventilated and lighted, and made a cozy temporary home for the new arrivals. There were stakes and wire netting and some long elm planks, and by the time they were called for supper, they had built a small run for Tinker, and a large cage for Nutmeg complete with an oak log and two branches of fir.

Joe was sleepy when he went to bed. The air was relaxing and the journey had tired him. But the new pajamas on his pillow woke him up. They were light blue with red piping, and on the breast pocket woven in red was an animal the image of Tinker. Mrs. Massiter had bought them for him. She must have known he was short on pajamas. He put them on and went downstairs again to thank her.

Mr. and Mrs. Potter had gone and she was locking the windows in the lounge.

She turned when he spoke.

"You look nice, Joe," she said. "The color suits you."

"They feel good." He was running his fingers over the silky lapel of the jacket. "But I'm not used to this sort." He pointed to the weaving on the pocket. "I like the weasel."

"I thought you would," she smiled. "You should sleep well in them."

"I don't know about that," Joe said. "I feel sleepy but I don't reckon I will."

"The storm shouldn't keep you awake." She smoothed down the curtain that had blown out over a chair before she closed the last window. "I don't think we shall get anything here."

"I'm not thinking about the storm," said Joe. "I'm wondering how Mr. Penny's getting on."

"I know," she said gently. "You've been thinking about him ever since we left London, haven't you?"

"I suppose I have, off and on."

"I saw your faces when you said good-by."

"It was taking the animals that did it," Joe said. "He'll be so lonely without them."

"Only for one night, Joe," she reminded him. "Tomorrow you'll be there. Besides, he still has Smokey and the cats."

"That's true."

She put her arm around his shoulder and walked him into the hall as far as the stairs.

"So you sleep well." She bent and kissed him lightly. "And we'll be on our way back in the morning."

Joe slept well until dawn, when the rain lashing his

window and a heavy roll of thunder awakened him with a start. The house seemed to shudder in the wind, and from his bed he could see the leaves hustling past his window. He got up and looked out.

The garden was a quagmire. The lawn was water-logged, the flowers beaten down into the soft mud of their beds. And the trees swayed and danced and shook like bedraggled puppets on invisible strings.

It was no better at breakfast time. The storm kept coming back. And it wasn't until mid-morning that the sky showed signs of any relief at all. That's when they started out. Mrs. Massiter preferred to wait until the violence had abated, although she knew Joe was restless to get away. But once they got going they wouldn't need to stop, for Mrs. Potter had made a thermos of coffee and had packed some sandwiches.

So they didn't stop. Yet it seemed a long way back to London. The country roads were wet and flooded in places; everywhere the storm had left a trail of damage. Even in the towns, roof slates were missing and some chimney pots had tumbled down. The water ran in the gutters, but the people had folded their umbrellas. The pavements and streets of London began to steam in the warming sun.

Joe's spirits rose as they jogged along Mile End Road and turned off at Whitecross Gate. It wasn't only seeing Mr. Penny, it was the thought of returning to do the job he'd planned to do before the weather broke. There was no wind now, the prospect was sunny. Maybe Mick Haggity would be back on the site. He'd seek him out

101 ✂

that afternoon. He could lose no more time. He'd have to corner Amber or Caution and climb the crane that night. . . .

But when they turned into Sparrow Street the crane wasn't there. Not where it should have been. There was a fire engine and a police car, and right in the yard a huge truck. There were people in uniform and people in overalls and just plain people.

Joe couldn't think what all the fuss was about, although he knew it must be serious. The billboard above the gates had gone. The one on which the pretty girl had advertised the Hippodrome. It had been swept into the yard as the enormous truck entered. But still he couldn't see what had happened. Not until Mrs. Massiter stopped the car and they had crossed to the gateway. Then they saw . . .

The tower crane was down.

Joe couldn't believe it. He could see the house now. Mr. Penny's house. And it had sunk in the middle like a badly cooked cake. The end of the jib had flattened it almost to the ground.

"Don't go in, Joe. Stay with me." The tight, shocked voice of Mrs. Massiter echoed in his ears. "I'll find out what happened. . . ."

Joe stayed with her. He couldn't go in. He was afraid. He heard the police inspector talking. He spoke quietly to Mrs. Massiter. Joe wasn't sure what he said . . . It seemed to be the storm . . . Lightning . . . And the wind . . . They'd found Mr. Penny . . . They'd taken him away in the ambulance . . . But he was dead . . . There would be an investigation . . . But he was dead . . . Mr. Penny— dead. . . .

There were bells in his ears now. It might have been a police car or another fire engine. He didn't know. All he was conscious of was the confusion. It didn't seem like Sparrow Street any more. . . .

He was grateful for Mrs. Massiter. She was something real and alive and warm to hold on to. The drive through the city was like a vague dream to him. But the numbness had gone when they reached the hotel. He was trembling when they went inside. Mrs. Massiter got the doctor and he gave Joe a sedative and he felt better when he was in bed. He was so drowsy he thought he would go to sleep. . . .

It was early when he awoke. But as soon as he got up and looked out of the window he knew where he was. He felt a lot better, although he remembered everything. And most of all he remembered Mr. Penny.

As he stared out across the square, a black cat stalked a sparrow in the grass and Joe suddenly thought of Caution and Amber and Smokey. Smokey must have been in his stable when it happened. Where was he now? In the confusion of yesterday the animals had been forgotten.

Joe got dressed and went downstairs. The clock over the reception desk was silently pointing to seven. It was quiet, like Sunday morning . . . It *was* Sunday morning. Joe had lost count of the days. There was no one in the hall except the clerk at the desk. Joe went boldly up to him.

"I'm with Mrs. Massiter," he said.

"I know, son." The clerk smiled. "I know all about you. What can I do for you first thing in the morning?"

103 ❧

"Give Mrs. Massiter a message, please. But not until she wakes up."

"Certainly."

"Tell her I've just gone down to Sparrow Street. She'll understand."

The clerk nodded and made a note on his pad.

"But don't disturb her."

"You can rely on me, son," the man said. "Is there anything else I can do?"

"Well," said Joe, "I haven't got any money. If you can let me have enough for the fare, Mrs. Massiter will give it back."

The clerk gave him ten bob and told him to change at Holborn and get the Twenty-five bus from there. Then he picked up the paper from under his desk and studied the picture of Saturday's scene on Sparrow Street.

Joe couldn't wait for the bus. He ran down Southampton Row. And when he saw a taxi turn in Theobalds Road he waved it to a stop. He'd never traveled in a taxi before, and all the way he kept his eye on the meter. But he needn't have worried for when the driver found out who he was and why he was going, he told him to skip the fare. The driver had read the papers, too.

Joe left the taxi at the top of the street and walked down to the yard. There was a policeman on the pavement near the injured wall of the house and he came toward him when Joe paused at the gates.

"Hello, laddie, I know your face," he said pleasantly. Joe glanced over the fence.

"Mr. Penny was my friend," he said quietly.

"I know. You're Joe." His face was solemn. "An awful

tragedy," he said. "Lucky you weren't there yourself, laddie."

"I've come to see about Smokey and the cats," Joe said. "I'd like to go in."

"Well, haven't seen any cats but I can tell you where the donkey is."

"He's all right?"

"Right as rain," said the policeman. "Tom Mason came around and took him to his place just after it happened."

"That's something," sighed Joe. "I was worried about him." He stepped nearer the gates, his eye catching the little wooden plaque announcing Mr. Penny's name and trade. "I was going in," he added.

"All right, laddie," the policeman agreed. "I reckon you're entitled to. But don't touch anything."

Joe went in. He was glad about Smokey. The stable doors were open, but apart from a hole in the roof, the sheds hadn't been damaged. The yard was empty save for little heaps of rubble, but the garden gate and woodshed had gone. One wall of the house was down and a lot of the roof had caved in, but the crane jib had been taken away. You could see where the trucks and hoists had been; their great tires had trampled the flowers and shrubs at the back of the house.

Joe walked around to the kitchen window and it wasn't there. The whole of the wall had collapsed in a mountain of rubble and there were bits of wallpaper and rags of curtain and broken crockery near the upturned sink. He bent down and scraped away a small heap of dust and plaster, and pulled something from underneath. He stood up, slowly turning it one way and then the other in his

105 ❧

hands. Then he took it with him into the yard.

As he walked slowly back to the gates a voice called to him from behind. He turned to find a stranger standing there.

"Hello," the man said. "You'll be Joe?"

"That's who I am," Joe said without interest.

"I've heard about you from your friend over there," he nodded toward the building site. "Mick Haggity."

Joe said nothing.

"I was here yesterday and talked to one or two people. And then I talked to Haggity. He told me about the garden and your friend Mr. Penny. And all you'd done here. He said you were fighting against the big boys to keep your piece of land."

"What's the difference now?" Joe muttered.

"I'm a writer. Heston Burke's my name. I write for the papers. I'd like to know more. Would you care to talk about it?"

"No," said Joe. "I don't want to talk about it now." He moved off toward the gates.

Burke watched him go. He'd witnessed many things, but this was something that would stay with him for the rest of his days. He didn't need any words. The picture would do. . . .

The broken house. The empty stable. A boy with a Panama hat.

· *Chapter Eleven* ·

Heston Burke started it. He wrote the story for the *Morning Express*. That's how the campaign got going.

The simple things . . . The fight of the little man who'd died for his beliefs . . . The council and the property men must have a change of heart . . . After this tragedy, surely a fitting memorial to a good and simple man was the preservation of his garden within the borough. . . . It was ironic, but it was the least that could be done. . . .

The story went over big, and every paper and newsreel

company joined in. Television, film, radio all featured the story and Sparrow Street went around the world. There were interviews and pictures at the Onslow Court Hotel, and for a few days Joe and Mrs. Massiter became the focus of attention at home and abroad. Even Smokey was photographed for the press and television before being sent to quieter pastures at Valley End.

Aunt Ethel and Liz in Brighton were very proud of Joe. So was Uncle Bert. It was good to know that he was on his way home at last.

The pressure and tension of living in the limelight began to tell on Joe and Mrs. Massiter, and toward the end of the week, after the funeral, they followed Smokey down to the country. It was peaceful at Valley End even if the telephone did ring sometimes, and the quiet atmosphere of the place, and having his own animals there with him, made it easier for Joe to put the excitement of those sad and hectic days behind him.

Until Mr. Massiter came.

Joe was in his new pajamas at the time. He'd had a bath and was just going to bed, and had come down to the lounge to wish Mrs. Massiter good night. That was the moment the Rolls-Royce arrived.

Mr. Massiter seemed subdued when he came into the house, and there was a stiff, formal atmosphere all over the lounge as his wife offered him a drink.

He took a sip and lit a cigarette, and it was almost a nervous gesture.

"I heard that Joe was with you," he said. "I wanted to see him."

"What have I done now?" Joe looked at him steadily.

He no longer felt afraid.

"Nothing to cause complaint, boy." He smiled faintly. It was the first time Joe had seen him smile. Perhaps it was the first time Mr. Massiter had for a long time. "I wanted to say how sorry I was—about Mr. Penny."

"You could have written a letter," Mrs. Massiter said coldly.

"I wanted to say it in person."

"How are you managing for time?"

"I managed to find enough to take a look at myself, Laura."

Joe felt he shouldn't be there. It was like listening outside the door. Only Mr. Massiter was different this time. Maybe because he was in his wife's house, or maybe he really was warm with sympathy and it had softened him a little. Or maybe there always had been a spark of tenderness buried under the hard exterior.

"Won't you join me in a drink, Laura?" he asked quietly. "There's something else I have to say."

"You have the floor, Arnold," she said, still cold. "You always did."

"Perhaps Joe would like a cordial," he suggested mildly.

"I'd like something," said Joe. "Please."

Mrs. Massiter returned to the cabinet then. She poured Joe a lemonade and a small gin and tonic for herself. And the three of them seemed to draw closer together in the center of the room.

"I don't know why we're all standing," Mrs. Massiter remarked.

"Let's stay where we are," her husband said. "I've something to show you." He took a slim roll of paper from inside his jacket. "Another good reason for my call this evening is that I wanted you both to know that in the plans we are drawing up for Sparrow Street, the council and our company have agreed to retain the garden. And in its new location it will be brought forward to the road, with the buildings set back on three sides of it." He unrolled the paper. "I haven't brought the actual plans with me," he went on, "but this sketch will give you an idea of the new setting."

They were still in the lounge when Joe went to bed. Mrs. Massiter had given her husband a final drink. But Joe had wished them both good night and had run up to his room to think. He wanted to consider the great new plan and he needed to be alone.

He sank into bed and stared at the ceiling and thought how the garden would look. Even if it was enclosed on three sides by tall buildings it would still need tending. Perhaps Joe would have the job when he grew up. Mr. Massiter would see to it. He was sure of that now. Maybe he could have his animals, or at any rate a donkey like Smokey, and a cart to take the weeds away. And a Panama hat. Just like Mr. Penny. Mr. Penny would have wanted it that way; he wouldn't have wished for anything to change. Joe was certain of that. So perhaps if he worked hard enough and wished hard enough everything could be the same as it always had been. . . . Which is a sad way to see things really for nothing is ever the same when you grow up.

But Joe didn't know that. And he had a long way to grow.

✿ About the Author

Geoffrey Morgan has lived for many years on a farm in Suffolk, England. He now divides his time between Suffolk and the town of Bexhill on the Sussex coast. A full-time writer, Mr. Morgan most enjoys sailing, meeting people, and looking over other people's boats.

In writing *A Small Piece of Paradise*, Mr. Morgan "thought the main aspect of this topical social problem concerned not the difficulty of rehousing or the compensation offered to the families concerned, but the feelings of the people themselves when faced with losing their homes. I have tried to describe what might have happened to one such home that lay across the path of 'progress.' "

A Note on the Type

This book was set on the Linotype in Janson, a recutting made direct from the type cast from matrices made by Anton Janson. Whether or not Janson was of Dutch ancestry is not known, but it is known that he purchased a foundry and was a practicing type-founder in Leipzig during the years 1660 to 1687. Janson's first specimen sheet was issued in 1675. His successor issued a specimen sheet showing all of the Janson types in 1689.

The general tone of Janson has a sturdiness and substance quite different from its predecessors. It is a highly legible type, and its individual letters have a pleasing variety of design. Its heavy and light strokes make it sharp and clear, and the full-page effect is characteristic and harmonious.

Text set in Janson
Composed by The Book Press, Inc., Brattleboro, Vermont
Printed by Halliday Lithograph Corp., West Hanover, Massachusetts
Bound by The Haddon Craftsmen, Inc., Scranton, Pennsylvania
Typography by Susan Detrich